"William Goodson tackles some critical issues of our time, with insight few others could match. Through his gracefully drawn characters and their intriguing journeys there is much to learn – while enjoying a great read. This is an important book that deserves widespread attention."

—Fran Moreland Johns
Author of *Dying Unafraid* and
Perilous Times

"...a coming-of-age story set in an ecologically distressed era ... in an elegant but straightforward prose that mimics Jack's constant struggle to understand the world around him ... "

—*Kirkus Reviews*

"... through all the ages of literature, story-telling has been used to tell basic truths and this book ... opens a whole new way forward for the environmental debate in a very accessible form..."

—Professor Philippa Darbre, PhD
University of Reading
United Kingdom

"... a novel that is more prophecy than science fiction ... an glimpse into what our future may be if we don't take steps to reverse releases of greenhouse gasses into the air and toxic chemicals into our environment."

—David O. Carpenter, MD
Institute for Health and the
Environment, University at Albany

"... not weighted down by excessive dystopian drama ... a tightly drawn novel about how ignorance and human procrastination can lead to a terrifying reality of climate catastrophe, species extinction, and epidemics."

—Ronald Piana
Freelance Science Writer
Co-author of *The Great Prostate Hoax*

"... an important contribution to the ongoing forensic and political debates about the injury to health and property from chemicals and pollutants in the environment."

—Michael Gilbertson, PhD
Occupational and Environmental
Health Research Group,
University of Stirling, Scotland

KOBB

Also by William Goodson

It's your body...Ask! (2000)

The Blue Eyed Girl (2014)

It's your body...Ask, Second Edition (2016)

KOBB

A novel by
William Goodson

RED SQUARE PRESS

KOBB

Publisher: Red Square Press
11331 Skyline Drive
North Tustin, CA 92715

ISBN 978-1-7327747-4-2

Edited by: Cyra McFadden, Laurie King
Cover Photo: Laura Vroman
Cover Design: Polly Lockman
Cover Portrait: Steele Douglas
Book Design: Jim Shubin, BookAlchemist.net

"In memory of lost opportunities."

Kelley's Bar
Kansas City, Missouri

September 1

"They'll never catch him."

"Huh?" Kobb replied. "Excuse me?" He'd been wandering in his own reverie, and he wasn't certain if the man at the next table had spoken to him.

"The other man. The terrorist. The one who rode off on a motorcycle," the guy continued.

Kobb had seen the sketch of his brother on the television screen above the bar. The police artist had conceptualized how Jack would have looked if he frowned; but Jack almost never frowned, so the picture made Kobb feel as if he was catching a glimpse of someone he should know, rather than his brother.

"Why not?"

"These terrorists. They're too well organized." The man continued, "You must've seen the news. There wasn't a shred of paper on the man. No record of fingerprints. Where do they find these people?"

"Don't know," Kobb replied.

"And it's weird how the rain started. Just as all those folks started dyin' from the air conditioners cuttin'out, it rains."

"Well, we certainly need the rain. What's it been? Nineteen months?"

"Yeah, but now all those environmental weirdos are sayin' the rain's 'cause the smoke has stopped. Almost like they did it on purpose."

"Don't know," Kobb said in an effort to escape the conversation.

The man rambled more as Kobb watched the face on the screen repeat the latest death toll from retirement centers in Arizona. Kobb feared to call his father. He would wait.

He looked around Kelley's. At other tables, customers also watched the evening news. "Although the plant itself is undamaged, it will be out of service for six months until repairs ..." Two men went through the motions of playing pool in the back.

Kobb caught other random words as a new television expert came on to discuss the manhunt: "... unable to provide a description of the second terrorist ... do not approach ... presumed to be armed and dangerous...."

Kobb didn't feel armed and dangerous. He felt sad and alone. His brother was gone, he hadn't anticipated hundreds of old folks dying from the heat, and his father was unlikely to survive in the desert without air conditioning.

Four Weeks Earlier

Kelley's Bar
Kansas City, Missouri

August 3

"… by a margin of 62 to 37 with one abstention."

Kobb looked up from his beer and watched the commentator pick up the story line from the Washington reporter. "Yielding to profound pressure from senior citizen groups, the Senate has effectively rejected the idea that the current drought is related to the increased burning of coal in the Four Corners Power Complex," the announcer continued before turning to his co-anchor.

"It's been a contentious issue, hasn't it, Carol?"

"Yes it has, David; and it's been the classic environmental conflict. There's no question that the seventeen-month drought has exceeded any previous experience. There's also the theory that emissions from increased generation of electric power, especially with fossil fuels such as coal, have warmed the troposphere and prolonged the drought."

She pointed to a chart. "Senior citizen groups, especially in the Southwest, have contested ..."

Kobb left a dollar tip and walked to the pay phone. He pushed the buttons.

"Dad, it's me."

"You saw the vote?" his father asked.

"Yeah."

"Not much to say, is there?"

"Dad ..."

"Kobb, don't worry about me. It'll be OK."

Kobb bit his lower lip. "I appreciate you saying that, Dad."

"I mean it, Son. Now do me proud."

"OK." Kobb paused for a breath. "'Bye, Dad."

"'Bye, Son. And God bless."

Kobb coasted down the incline by Kelley's. As the old Honda gained inertia, he popped the clutch; the engine jerked and began to sputter. At the corner of Westport Road, he curled his wrist to release the clutch again and revved the engine. When the traffic cleared, he turned right and headed west.

He crossed the Kaw River on the turnpike. Except where moisture collected in the shadow of bluffs, the ground was parched and cracked. The few stalks of corn that had managed to sprout had stopped at knee height.

Dust devils whirled between the remnants of a crop. Kids played hide and seek in the sultry heat. The humidity still surprised Kobb. No matter how much wind blew through his open shirt, he was drenched in his own sweat.

On Main Street in Council Grove, the bank thermometer said "104." Two women shared an umbrella to protect themselves from the heat.

The cafe was dark inside. He ordered a hamburger and asked for the phone. He would not make this call on his cell phone.

There were thirty rings before Kobb heard Jack's distinctive twang over the phone. "HEH-lc," as Jack's voice dropped between syllables.

"Jack? It's me."

"How's it going, buddy?"

"Did you see the TV?"

"Nope, I was working the calves. Do that to music."

"They voted it down."

"Shit! You talk to Dad?"

"Yep."

There was a long silence.

"Look, I'm in Council Grove. I'll be there in about two hours."

"OK. Be careful."

"I always ride careful, Bro."

Southwest Kansas

August 4

Mountain oysters sizzled in the pan. "You know how much cholesterol is in those things?" Kobb asked.

Jack smiled and ignored his implication. "Yeah, but it reminds me of makin' steers with dad when we were kids. Think of it as comfort food."

"Comfort food!? All I can think of is those little bull calves that just been made into steers." Kobb shifted the crotch of his jeans. "Makes me very un-comfortable."

"Hell, Kobb, I'm not going to live long enough to worry about cholesterol." And then more seriously he added, "Hardly enough to make a good fry anyway. We lost most of the calves this year. Cows just couldn't hold them. You know, the heat. No water.

"The aquifer is down another sixteen feet in the last two years," he continued. "Everyone taking water, no rain. Water's deeper, more electricity to pump it out, more fuel burned up. It's that damned cycle you keep talking about. Saving gas saves water. Or is that backwards?"

Kobb watched Jack wrap himself up and get confused

in what he was saying. Such a difference the meningitis had made. "Something like that, little brother. Something like that."

Kobb was ten minutes older so he'd always called his twin "little brother."

Cortez, Colorado

August 5

The teenager took Kobb's ten-dollar bill and counted back the change. Kobb glanced at a car through the window in the front of the lobby as he balanced a large popcorn and two sodas and backed through the door into the theater. It was dark inside, and the previews had already begun.

Jack was sitting on the aisle, half way down on the right side. He half stood and took one soda as Kobb stepped across him into a seat. He mouthed his first handful of popcorn, but immediately stopped chewing and looked at Kobb. "You didn't put any butter on it."

"No."

"Why not?"

"I didn't want butter."

"You know I like butter."

"It's not butter, Jack. It's butter flavoring in palm oil. That stuff is shit for your arteries."

"Kobb, I like the taste." And with that, Jack stalked out to the concession stand.

Kobb watched him leave. No one ever wondered if they were twins anymore. He'd learned in school how meningitis could have lasting effects. Jack being sick had made a lot of difference.

"Tell me again," Jack asked after the movie. "Why're we just going for a pipe? Why not the whole thing?"

Kobb took a sip on his beer before he answered. "I've been thinking about that plant and looking at the satellite photos. There's so much security I can't figure a way to harm the plant, but it needs coal to keep going. If we break the coal pipe I figure they'll run out within a few days. It'll take them at least six months to get it going again."

Jack was confused. "Coal pipe? You mean conveyor belt or something, don't you? Coal can't go anywhere in a pipe."

"But that's my point. Coal does go in pipes. I read about it in a book one time. They grind coal and mix it with water.

It's called a slurry and it pumps just like oil."

Jack thought for a few minutes while he absorbed the idea of a pipe running with coal. "So how'd you find the pipe, anyway?"

"Satellite photos."

"Satellite photos?"

"I got the idea on a flight from Las Vegas to Texas," Kobb explained. "I was looking at hills. You know, with the layers of rock and the folds from earthquakes. Anyway, I saw this line that went straight across hills and valleys. It didn't match the other lines. Didn't fit."

Kobb took another sip on his beer.

"You can see those things. The things that don't fit. That's how they find some of those old archeology ruins.

"Anyway, in the pictures online, I see there's a valley south of the number three generator. Once you see the pipe go in that direction, you just look for the scars on the hills. Then I realized it was the pipe, the coal pipe."

"So how'd you follow it, the pipe? Rent a plane?"

"Nope. Satellite photos again. It's all free on the Internet."

"That's clever, big brother."

Kobb watched the television screen flash between images as Jack flicked the remote until they both fell asleep. The beds in the motel were comfortable.

Northwest New Mexico

August 6

Jack shook the can of diesel fuel to get the last drops. Clouds had cleared and a half moon cast shadows on the asphalt and small desert plants. They worked in silence and without a flashlight. Kobb glanced at the Big Dipper; for a moment, he remembered when his dad had first explained how the two stars at the end of the cup pointed to the North Star.

Jack settled the lids back on each drum. He took care not to make sudden movements. Then he took a big breath and sighed.

Kobb watched as his brother turned and looked at him. For a moment, he held his breath, but he also remembered that his father had confirmed the plan.

Jack did not look back at his brother before returning to the truck and starting the engine.

Kobb pulled the tarp over the drums and stepped over his motorcycle.

Jack was down the entry ramp as Kobb coasted the motorcycle and popped the clutch. After the engine caught, he stopped and waited.

The bridge was two miles from the entry ramp. Jack held a steady fifty miles per hour. Kobb could see his taillights. He was to wait until Jack stopped and put on his flashers in the middle of the bridge. They did not want a passing motorist to associate a lingering motorcycle with the truck.

The bridge had a slight incline and Kobb missed the brake lights since the truck almost stopped by itself. When the flashers started, he revved his engine and fish-tailed slightly where loose gravel covered the pavement.

There were no cars going either way.

Jack stepped away from the back of the truck and started laying the trigger wire behind him as he walked toward the end of the bridge they had come from. "Hey, Kobb. Where you been?" he called out as his brother approached.

"Screw you. Let's go."

Kobb circled the bike and started back toward the same end of the bridge. As he went, he reached into a satchel and pulled out warning flares. They were already open; each one flashed into fire in a split second, and he quickly approached the end of the bridge.

It was then that the trooper turned on his red lights.

The trooper, however, must have been looking up the road because he rolled down the window on the passenger side. "What's happen'n fellas?"

"Oh, my brother's truck broke down."

"Need help? I can call for a tow."

"No. No." Kobb scrambled for an excuse. "I think it's just gas. The gauge is broken so he carries a can in the back for when he runs out. It'll just be a minute."

"You can't see those flares too well. I'll stay with my lights until you get going."

Kobb had eased back so that the officer had to look back a bit to see him. Behind the officer, he could see that Jack had run back up the bridge to cock the sawed off shotgun that was to set off the explosion. "Fuck," he said under his breath as the officer took the initiative and drove toward the middle of the bridge.

From a hundred yards away, Kobb watched as Jack left the rear of the truck and started back toward him. The officer slowed as though to wave as he passed Jack. He seemed to think that there was someone else with the truck.

Jack broke into a run.

The officer pulled even with the truck and put on his spotlight.

Light flashed on the empty cab, then back and settled on the wire.

The trooper's car backed up so that he could flash his spotlight on the open bed of the truck.

Then Kobb heard a loudspeaker squawk from the car. "Stop."

The trooper backed the car toward Jack. He swerved

slightly as he tried to accelerate in reverse. Jack paused, looked back, and pulled the wire; and it happened just as Kobb had expected: There was a tiny flash before a ball of fire. Speeding in reverse, the trooper's car swerved and hit the rail of the bridge. Kobb glimpsed Jack's silhouette against the glare of exploding diesel oil.

Flames from unexploded oil outlined the end of the bridge; and the trooper and his car settled from sight into the fire.

Miraculously, Kobb saw Jack crawl to his feet and stagger toward him.

The motorcycle engine never stopped. Kobb skidded in a circle and sped out onto the stump of the span to where Jack staggered, dazed by the explosion. "Come on, little brother. Let's get out of here."

Jack stared blankly at Kobb.

"Come on ..." Kobb yelled.

Jack tried to straighten himself.

"Shit!" Kobb rolled the bike back so he was beside Jack. "Come on, Jack." But Jack ignored Kobb's words. "Can you hear me?" Kobb shouted. "Let's go."

The smell of burning oil was increasing. Smoke obscured the moon to the west. Jack looked puzzled and stood with his arms limp at his sides as if to ask, "What?"

Kobb reached out and took Jack's shoulder and pulled him toward the motorcycle. Finally Jack responded, but he got on in slow motion.

Kobb waited a moment for Jack to put both arms around his waist, then revved the bike and started back down the road. As he accelerated off the end of the bridge he saw headlights approaching. They were big lights, high in the air, like on a truck. The unseen driver seemed to sense that that somehow they were responsible for the fire and were trying to escape. He turned the side of his rig to block both lanes.

Kobb was speeding now, but the road wasn't an option. In a split second he turned for the median. He heard the driver call something like "mother fucker" as he bounced into the gully between the strips of concrete. They bounced more than he expected; he almost lost control, and abruptly the motorcycle got lighter.

"Oh, god." Kobb realized Jack had lost his grip. He'd already started up the opposite embankment and when he let off the gas; the bike stopped on the spot. Jack was lying behind him at the bottom of the gully no more than fifty yards from the trucker. Another truck stopped behind the first one.

Kobb edged his way down the mixed sand and dirt of the embankment, dodging small cacti. The truckers had flashlights and were shouting, "You son of a bitch. Fuckin' terrorists." But they hesitated, and Kobb reached his brother first.

Jack didn't move when Kobb pulled his arm. Then he moaned and tried to put his hand up to shake off Kobb's grip. "Kobb..." but he couldn't move.

"Come on, Jack."

Jack did not try to move.

The truckers cautiously looked for a way to work their way down the slope. "Jack!" Kobb shouted. Jack choked and coughed blood. Then Kobb realized that Jack was pulling at his own trousers. He rolled Jack so that his hand was free, and Jack lifted his hand holding his wallet. With effort, he motioned for Kobb to take it. "No fingerprints," he whispered.

"What?"

"Take it with you. I've never had fingerprints."

Phoenix, Arizona

August 7

The old Honda shone in the afternoon sun. Kobb had wiped it down with nail polish remover and applied a coat of wax to every surface. A kid who was watching him had asked, "Why you wearin' gloves, mister?"

He'd answered that it was to keep the wax off his fingers.

"My dad don't worry 'bout wax on his fingers. Mom says she likes the smell. Makes her know that dad's been takin' care of the car." Kobb had smiled and kept polishing.

It wasn't unusual for someone to polish a bike on a residential street. He'd hoped all afternoon that no one would notice that he didn't live in the neighborhood. There were a lot of apartments, however, and no one had said a thing.

The kid stopped asking questions, but didn't wander far away.

"Hey," Kobb called to him. "Can I ask your name?"

"Roger. What's yours?"

Kobb had prepared for this. "Jack. So Roger, do you want to make a couple of bucks?"

"What I gotta' do?"

"I'm going to go do some grocery shopping," he replied. "I want someone to make certain no one messes up my wax job. You do that?"

"Sure."

Kobb gave him two dollars in quarters before he pulled off the gloves. He had wiped them, too.

As he turned the corner, he waved to the kid. Then he hopped a bus.

The air in the room stifled Kobb's breathing. His shirt was wet from sweat, and he wanted a glass of water. He guessed that the temperature was about 95° "Dad, I can get you out of here."

"Where to, Kobb? Where to?"

"I'll take you up to Flagstaff. It's cooler up there, 75 or so."

His dad changed the conversation. "You know, I wonder sometimes how they did it before the air conditioners. The heat you know. I heard on the news that they had some heat in New York City, the century before last, where a hundred people a day died from it. Besides, I wanted this anyway, didn't I?"

"Dad," Kobb cautioned as he looked around the room full of equally elderly persons, also suffering in the heat.

His dad replied in a stage whisper, "Don't worry. They won't hear, and the help here is too stupid to understand what you're saying." He waved a hand at the television in the corner. "They're saying it was terrorists. They talk about Jack a lot, 'Terrorist John Doe Number One;' but they don't know who he is. Last thing they said he was a Venezuelan agent trying to boost the price of oil. At least they figured out it was someone trying to shut down the Four Corners plant."

He lowered his voice and looked into Kobb's eyes. "Go home, Kobb. Tell them you got worried when this terrorist thing happened. You were out visiting me. You shaved your beard because it was cooler. Hope that it rains. If it does, finish school, have a family. Think well of us. Know that you did the right thing."

"Dad, stop it."

"No regrets, Kobb." His father shook his head and held up his hand. "I encouraged you, because I was too weak to do it myself. It was me as much—no—maybe more than you. It was a tough job and, well, hell, you know how that the rest of that stupid line goes."

Kansas City, Missouri

September 1

Kobb took a bus home. Home if he could call it that. Jack's illness had inspired him to go to medical school, but Jack was gone so learning to help his brother was irrelevant. Kobb felt irrelevant, but he went through the steps preparing to start his third year clinical rotations in a few days, right after Labor Day. Bought his white coat and signed the papers for the next year of student loans. He couldn't tell his classmates what he'd done on vacation. He was an older student, so no one really knew him at the med center, or guessed what he was capable of doing if it was necessary, or more specifically, if it was the right thing to do because nothing else would work.

The drunk at the next table, and the incessant news references to his brother as John Doe Number One, didn't help. The only relief was stepping over the torrent of water in the gutter in front of the apartment where he lived alone. The water from the rain that proved he was right, even if what he'd done was so wrong. And there was Kelley's. Another beer at Kelley's.

The sound of the rain increased as the door opened. A tall blonde entered and shook the water from her hair. Then she looked around the room.

Her face changed with recognition, and she walked toward Kobb.

Kobb was surprised. He didn't recognize her.

Then the man at the next table stood and intercepted her with a hug. After a long moment, he pushed back from her. "You're soaked."

"I don't care," she replied. "It's such wonderful weather."

Forty Years Later

North Central Nebraska

Two or three times a night, as I lie beside my wife, I feel one or sometimes both of our twins kick in her stomach. The first time she felt them, she jumped in surprise and had me hold my hand on her to feel what she felt, but they stayed silent to my touch for a long time. Now, she feels them so often that she no longer comments on the sensations. But for me, they are always a miracle, and no matter how her pregnancy turns out, no matter how perfectly or imperfectly they are formed, I will only love them more when I can hold them, more than I love them now as they lie just inches from me, playing their game of kicking their mother and then kicking each other.

I know how important it will be for them to feel accepted, because I know how horrible it is growing up when something makes you feel different.

My name is Jack Kobb. I live with my wife in the house my parents bought just before I was five years old. My father is Perseus Kobb. For years he told me he was named for the Perseid Meteor Shower that comes every summer after his birthday, but not long ago I learned he was named after his father and my dad's full name is Perseus Kobb, Junior.

Kobb is one of those names that guys like to yell across the room, or across a field, so I get called Kobb a lot. But it turns out I wasn't the first one in my family to be called Kobb. My grandfather, the first Perseus Kobb, was known to everyone simply as Kobb. That's why Dad dropped the junior and became Percy Kobb, which is how I knew him as I grew up. I also wasn't the first person in my family named Jack, but that's getting ahead of myself.

When I first moved to this house with my parents, all of the rooms were empty from wall to wall, and it seemed huge. It was built for a gentleman farmer, a successful businessman from Omaha, who'd wanted a country place that he could expense as a business raising cattle. But he hadn't counted on the drought and the water table dropping to virtually unreachable levels so that there was only enough water to raise two or three cows on a place that used to support a whole herd.

Mom and dad bought the house for a price that was essentially a giveaway. Trees turned brown by July, and the wife of the man from Omaha had long since determined that they would get rid of the place. Besides my parents, no one else wanted to buy it. It made sense for us because Dad had income other than raising scrawny cows. He worked as the primary care doctor in the region. The government didn't want everyone to move out, so they subsidized his practice, just like they provided satellite lessons for home schooling and kept a post office open for fewer than a thousand people.

The house was intended to entertain many guests, and it had six bedrooms and five bathrooms. My parents decided I would use a room on the second floor across the hall from them. I immediately found that the other door in my bedroom led to a bathroom and another bedroom on the other side led back to the hall. Once I learned I could run around in a circle through the rooms, I was happy, but Mom was not.

"Whoa, whoa, whoa," she called. She explained that we would leave the door closed to what I thought would be my bathroom, and when I was upstairs, I would go across the hall and use the toilet that was off their room. She didn't say it, but this way she wouldn't get stuck keeping another bathroom clean. I went to the toilet at night by going through their bedroom.

That arrangement lasted until I came in to use the toilet one night and Mom was making a lot of noises. The next day, she opened the door to the bathroom off my room and cleaned the toilet and sink. "I think you're old enough to have your own bathroom. Now you won't need to come through Dad's and my room at night," she said. "But you still need to put the toilet seat down after you pee." I tried to remember to put the top of the toilet seat down after I peed, but I got confused when to put the seat up and when to put it down, so like most boys I saw my age, I sat down for everything. It was easier.

I have two memories from before we moved to this house. In one, I look up at green leaves blowing in a breeze. There are flickers of light and traces of blue sky beyond the leaves, but there is no glare of sunlight in my eyes to make me uncomfortable. The source of this memory, if indeed it is real, puzzles me because all of my life that I'm sure I remember has been in a place that is dry and has only single trees. No one has told me this, but I have come to assume those trees were in Omaha.

The other memory is more of a sense of situation than an exact memory. I am lying on my back. Two women, one with brown hair and one with no hair, and two men, one with dark hair and one with gray hair remove my diaper to look at me. They seem anxious, or at least they discuss what to do about me, or with me. There is no photograph like this, so I know it is a memory, but I see it as a picture in which I am the fifth person captured by the photographer. I trust these adults, and feel safe lying on the table with them standing around me.

The men, first one and then the other, touch me where my diaper was removed. It might have been pleasurable, but the adults frown, and I wonder what I did to upset them. I wish I could make it better, but I don't know what to do.

I blink, and the woman with no hair is gone. I blink a second time, and the man with gray hair is gone, too.

The first time I recollected this scene I was sure the woman and the man who stayed were my parents. I was much older before I knew the names of the woman with no hair and the gray-haired man.

Every other childhood memory is from our ranch in north central Nebraska. I see the unending brown dirt that swirls on most days. I chase chickens in the farmyard, and I dig for worms. There are no photographs to suggest such activities to me, but I can look out the window any day and see all of these things, so I know they are real.

My father grew up in Kansas City and went to medical school in Omaha. After his internship, he volunteered for the Indian Health Service and was posted to the Pine Ridge Reservation in South Dakota.

He met Mom just before he started his two years in the Indian Health Service, and on one of her visits to his trailer on the reservation, I was conceived. They lived on the reservation until she was past her seventh month.

That was when the epidemic was being whispered about, and she wanted to go back to Omaha in case there was a problem with me. Dad pleaded hardship and was allowed extended leave from the Health Service after he promised to return to the area at some time in the future.

They stayed in Omaha while Dad got training in family medicine. He learned how to care for minor trauma and broken bones and how to deliver babies. Then, with my mother's agreement, they moved back to Northern Nebraska. Dad wasn't in the Indian Health Service this time, but it was an area of need so the Public Health Service sent him there.

From my earliest life, I knew something was unique about me—and that did not mean unique in a good way—and that Mom felt responsible. She never left me alone with a babysitter who came to our house specifically to care for me. She would leave me with the woman with no hair so she must have been safe, but I was so small that I didn't know how she fit into my life. I felt Mom was both trying to hide and trying to compensate for something, hoping the same action would accomplish both. She had always been a woman who dreamed of returning to a city—New York until that wasn't possible—but she agreed to move to rural Nebraska to get away from the stress of hiding me.

When we first moved to Nebraska, before my parents bought a house, they rented a trailer, much like their trailer on the Pine Ridge Reservation. They thought it was romantic. It was not long, however, before they realized that the isolation also solved a problem they had not known how to address. It was an area the rest of the country pretty much forgot, where they would not stand out except by being there. But that was okay because everyone there was odd or unusual for the reason that they lived there at all.

I never heard Dad talk about moving to another place, but there was always the sense that he'd left someone behind and he was waiting for them to catch up. Occasionally, mostly at night when the air was very still, you could hear a motorcycle on the highway that went past, out of sight from our house. Dad would stop whatever he was doing and watch our dirt road to see if anyone had turned off the pavement to come up to our house, and he always seemed disappointed when you could tell from the sound of the engine that the biker was accelerating up the hill on the main road, going north, and away from us.

There weren't enough people living around us for dad to have a big practice. Anyone who lived closer to Valentine or Mitchell or Chamberlain usually went there. Still, there were just under a thousand people living within thirty to forty miles, many of whom liked to be treated close to home, and almost all of whom liked my dad's affable smile and way of putting everyone at ease. But Dad was bored a lot of the time.

The first spring on the ranch, he got real excited to help the local vet, Dr. Porter. Doc Porter, as everyone called him, had practiced there his whole life. After the water dropped and cattle herds were sold off, he'd stayed on because he had nowhere else to go. The doc often dropped by and chatted with my dad. They were the closest things to colleagues that either one of them had. One doctor took care of the few cows that were left, and one doctor took care of the few people who had hung on.

I'd listen to them as they sat at the table and talked, and after awhile they'd forget I was there. Dad talked about a breech delivery, and Doc Porter talked about a breech calf. This led to a discussion of working cattle. I didn't know what that meant. I thought you milked cows and got meat, but working them made no sense.

While I was trying to figure that out, Doc Porter exclaimed, "Heck, I'm working calves at Cy's place on Friday. Why don't you come over?"

Dad liked the idea, and said he'd be there by 8:30. It was summer, so he'd have plenty of time to do chores after sunup. On Friday, however, Mom was feeling ill. She didn't take her morning run, and she didn't want to spend the day trying to take care of me.

"I told Porter I'd be there," Dad argued.

"Well," she told him, "you can't expect Jack to sit on his thumbs all day. You take him with you."

That wasn't Dad's plan. "But he'll be bored there, too. I can't let him just hang around. Even the three-month calves are double his size. He can get hurt …"

But Mom was insistent, and in the end, we half-walked, half-ran to Cy's place because the arguing had made us late.

Cy's place was like ours, a couple of hundred acres of mostly dry ground with a few trees. If you drove to his house, you went west from ours for a mile to the highway, north for a mile, east for two miles, and south on his road for just under a mile.

If you walked, you went across a creek bed that was almost always dry except after a big rain. Other times there were only a few puddles that hung on in the shade. Going directly to Cy's place took only twenty minutes and was about three-quarters of a mile, though admittedly there was a bit of a challenge in the two hills we had to cross.

Doc Porter saw me right away. "Starting him early?" he asked with a smile.

"Sally's sick or something," Dad explained. "Anyway, if he's going to start the trade …" he joked with a shrug.

In addition to Cy's three calves, there were two owned by another farmer I'd never seen. He had a son my size named Ronnie. That was one of the first times I met a guy my age from one of the surrounding farms. Usually we stayed around our homes.

Working the calves was old hat to Ronnie. He'd been around his father and cattle from before he could remember. After we talked a little, he acted like I was okay and led me to a hayloft where we could look down on my dad, his dad, and Doc Porter.

The men led calves one at a time into a narrow metal pen and before the calf could turn around they pressed in the side of the pen to hold it in place. My dad drew up a big syringe, bigger than anything I'd seen before, that was for the vaccinations.

"This is how they make steers," said Ronnie as he pointed to Doc Porter who reached between the calf's legs from behind. I didn't follow what happened, but he used one hand to pull something out that was attached by a little white string, like a long noodle or worm. With a quick move, Doc cut the worm, my dad gave the vaccinations in the calf's butt, Ronnie's dad released the press, and the calf bucked slightly a few times to adjust to the new reality of its life. Dad slapped the butt of the calf as it wandered out. "Sorry, fella," he said.

Doc took what he held in his hand and put it in a pan by his side. "Those are the oysters," said Ronnie to show off his knowledge. "There aren't as many calves as there used to be, but if we stay out of their way, we all get some."

"Get some?" I asked.

"Yeah. Cy grills them fresh. I like them with Tabasco sauce."

—m—

We walked home as it was getting dark. The oysters had been okay, but I felt bloated and was glad for the walk. Dad said Mom would have dinner ready, but that didn't sound appealing at all.

"Sally," Dad called out as we walked into the house. No one answered, but I didn't think anything of it and went to the kitchen for a glass of water as dad went upstairs.

Before the glass was full, I heard dad shout from upstairs, "Jack, come up here right away!" I ran up the stairs to their room. Dad was with Mom. She was pale, and there was blood on their sheets and on the floor toward the bathroom. He spoke precisely in a voice that demanded I not ask questions.

"Call 9-1-1. Use my special phone. Give them our location and tell them we have a class one emergency. Need medevac. Hemorrhaging miscarriage."

"What kind of carriage?"

"One word, MISS-CARRIAGE," he repeated clearly and carefully. "They'll understand. Then call Cy. Tell him what I told you to tell the medevac. Tell him I need him here. When you've done that, bring my bag in the front hall."

It was fully dark by the time I'd called Cy. He had a four-wheel drive ATV, and pretty soon I could see and then hear him driving over the same path we had used to walk home. The medevac helicopter got there at almost the same time.

The paramedics rushed past me up to Mom and Dad's room. I watched from the door, ignored by the adults. One paramedic cut Mom's shirt, slopped brown disinfectant on her bare shoulder, and used a thing like a hand-held power drill to put a screw into her bone.

My mouth went dry, but I couldn't look away. I was certain the screw in her shoulder would really hurt, but Mom's eyes stayed closed and she had no expression.

"Done," the paramedic said to her partner.

The partner pushed on a bag of water, and said, "It's running great. Let's roll."

The first paramedic dropped the drill back in her bag and reached for their stretcher. It seemed like hours, but they were ready to go only a few minutes after they got to my parents' room. My dad told me later that the drill to put water into her bone marrow was the fastest way to get emergency access for an IV, and it probably saved Mom's life.

Dad and Cy helped the paramedics get Mom on a stretcher, and they all started down the stairs. At the front door, Dad turned and handed Cy a small bundle. "Keep this for now. Can Jack stay at your place? I'll be back as soon as I can and clean this up."

"Sure," said Cy. He put one hand on my shoulder, held the bundle in his other hand, and led me outside.

We followed from a distance until they finished loading Mom in the helicopter. Dad ran back to hug me. "Mom's going to be all right, but she needs more than I can do right now. You stay with Cy and Martha."

Then he ran to the helicopter. Ducking under the blades, he climbed in, and the engine noise dropped to a deeper level before they rose into the air.

I could hear the whap, whap, whap of the helicopter for a minute or so after they had passed over the hill. I guessed they were going to Valentine this time.

Cy made me put on a seatbelt for the ride back to their place. I remember jerking around a lot and catching on the seat belt, but I didn't hold on. I could have bumped out and I wouldn't have noticed. Mom looked dead, and all Dad said was to promise that he'd be back. There were no words I could put together to express my fear and loneliness that night.

Martha was all chatty as soon as we got there. "So nice you can stay with us. You're dad'll be back before you know it." But she kept looking at the bundle in Cy's hand, until he saw her looking at it and put it in their refrigerator. It wasn't that late, but Martha had me go to bed in a room next to theirs. She and Cy didn't try to explain anything more than what Dad had said. I couldn't sleep, and I didn't even know yet that was the night I became an only child.

I love the word cloudburst. It's the image of a cloud getting so full of rain that it bursts and drops all its water at one time. The science teacher on the satellite school says that water evaporates and rises into the air, but the upper air gets so warm from the sun shining on bits of dust and engine exhaust, that more and more water accumulates high in the top of clouds. Finally, some unknown thing triggers one drop of water to condense out of all that humidity up there, and all of a sudden, there are more drops than you could imagine, and they all fall at once. The more dirt and exhaust in the air, the warmer the tops of cloud get, the longer water accumulates before it falls down, and the bigger the mess when the cloud bursts.

Mom was in the hospital for about a week. Dad came home a few nights, but it was a three-hour drive. He had me stay with Cy and Martha because, even when he was home, he was gone a lot and I'd be in the way in at the hospital.

The day Mom came home there was a cloudburst to end all cloudbursts. The dry creek between our house and Cy and Martha's swirled over the bank and took out the last of the fence that used to mark off whose cattle were whose back when there were so many cattle that it wasn't easy to know just by looking at the individual animals.

Mom and Dad picked me up before they went home so it was a homecoming for Mom and me at the same time. The storm ended as we arrived. There were still clouds over us, but it was clear in the west where the weather came from. A long glow lingered over the hill behind our house, and the wind blew the clouds on east before it finally got dark.

Mom was not as pale, but she still needed Dad to help her up the stairs. He and I brought our food upstairs to eat dinner with her.

Usually there was a haze in the sky even as far out in the country as where we lived, but the cloudburst washed out the haze and the sky was crystal clear. Even though everything was muddy, Dad wanted to go outside to look at stars after Mom was asleep. "There's a story for almost every set of stars," he said. "The neat thing is how the Greeks taught the Europeans one set of stories and the people in America had a whole different set of stories for the very same stars."

We had done this before, but in the past I felt like I was part of a class with many students that he would be teaching over time. He would show me, but I was a step along the way. He would show others after me, and he reserved some of his energy for future students. The night Mom came back, I was the only person in the whole world, and he taught me alone.

Dad turned off the barnyard light before we went outside and used a big flashlight to point to a whitish band, like a sort of cloud that ran from north to south. "That's the Milky Way," he said. "Actually, it's most of the rest of our galaxy that we see from where we are."

He kneeled and drew a big circle in the dirt. Then he put a little "x" at one side. "The big circle is our galaxy." He pointed to the "x" at the side of the circle. "We're here at the very edge. When we see the Milky Way, all those stars that look like a cloud, we're really looking into the middle of all of our galaxy."

"Why's it called the Milky Way?" I asked.

"A long, long time ago, people could see the sky clear every night there weren't clouds. They thought this looked like a wisp of milk spilled in the sky."

"Spilled?"

"Spilled by the people who lived above the sky, they thought." He let the idea that people lived above the stars sink in. "Humans have always thought someone lived up there. That's why they name the constellations."

I'd heard this from him before, and each time he came back to the different stories for the Big Dipper. The Greeks called it the Big Bear, and that became Ursa Major in Latin in Rome. The tribes of the Pacific Northwest saw it as a bear chased by a brave, a woman, and their dog. The middle star of the handle of the dipper is really two stars, and they could tell who had exceptional vision by who could see what they called a papoose on the back of the woman.

I was proud that I could see the second smaller star in the middle of the handle.

The Lakota—Dad was careful to call the tribe at Pine Ridge by their name for themselves—saw the pole constellation as a coyote. In their traditional beliefs, Coyote with a capital "C" had been responsible for creating much of the earth that we lived on.

I tried to understand what a coyote was, but they were gone now because they'd been hunted to extinction by ranchers who thought getting rid of coyotes would save their cattle business. But loss of water was the real cause, and killing coyotes didn't bring more rain ... or save their cattle.

For my next birthday, Dad found some stickers shaped like stars to put on the ceiling of my room. He explained that they picked up energy when the light was on in the room, and after the light was off they glowed for an hour or so. He made it sound like they were little savings banks to hold light and then give it back. We arranged them like the Big Dipper, the Little Dipper, and other constellations.

Two days after mom got home from the hospital, a car came up the road going slow, so as not to raise a cloud of dust. There was some fine print on the door, but it parked too far away for me to see the letters, and I didn't read well yet anyway. My dad, however, seemed to know who they were, and he stepped outside onto the porch and closed the door behind him.

I watched through the window. The man was in a uniform and had a gun, but he wasn't from the sheriff or the State Patrol. The woman held a black book and a black notebook to her chest. Her shirt was buttoned up to her neck despite the hot day, and I couldn't help but stare at her cross necklace.

Mom wore a small cross on a gold chain. "It was a gift from my mother," she'd told me. I could always tell when Mom was thinking about something serious because she'd hold the cross in her hand and rub it with her thumb for a long time before she spoke. But this woman's cross was gigantic and made of dark wood and hung from a strip of leather as big as a horse bridle.

I couldn't hear what she said to Dad, but I could tell he was pretty upset. He didn't swear, but he swore now, loud enough that I heard despite the closed door. "Why in hell would I do that?" The woman said something and my dad shouted, "Like hell you will."

The officer stepped between the woman and my dad and said something that got him to settle down, but Dad was still angry as they came into the house. "Jack," my dad said, "this woman wants to talk to you. I want to tell her to go to hell, but the officer says I need to let her talk to you."

I looked at her and my dad. She turned to him and said, "We need to talk alone." And when my dad didn't move, she added, "You need to step outside." Dad looked at the officer and then stepped into the next room.

The woman suggested we sit down, and then she opened her black notebook and asked me to tell where I'd been the day my mom got sick.

"With my dad, over at Cy and Martha's."

"How long were you there?"

"Almost to dark," I answered.

"And what did you do that took you so long, all day?" she asked skeptically.

"Made steers."

"Made steers?" she challenged me.

"You know. You give a calf a shot and pull out its white worm and it's a steer."

The officer realized that the woman had no idea what

I was talking about and could hardly keep a straight face.

"And that's all?" she asked.

"No. We grilled the oysters, too. They were okay, but I don't think I'll eat them next time. My stomach didn't feel too good afterwards."

The officer laughed out loud. When the woman glared at him, he forced himself to stop laughing, but he winked and cracked a grin at me to let me know I was okay.

"So tell me." The woman straightened her notebook and the black book on the table before she continued. "Do you have any brothers or sisters?"

"No."

"Would you like to have a little brother or a little sister?"

"Yes."

"And do you know that what your mother and father did means that you'll never have a brother or sister?"

I had no idea how she could know this. The officer was shocked she had asked the question. And my dad burst into the room. I guess he'd been listening through the door. "That's it. Get out," he shouted.

"Mister Kobb," the woman said, "I have a right to be here. I have a duty to be here ..."

Dad cut her off. "I've told you everything you need to know."

"I've heard your story, of course, but I need to hear

your son in his words, too." She patted the black book on the table and added, "As the Psalmist says, 'Out of the mouths of babes ...'"

"Yes, and the same book says, 'Let your nay be nay ... love thy neighbor ... turn the other cheek ...' and asks if a father would give his son a stone if he asked for bread. I am honest with my son. Don't give me your pious bullshit. You knew you were barking up the wrong tree after I answered your first question."

"Mister Kobb, I have a right to ask ... "

"No! You have a right to ask questions." He looked at the officer and then back to the woman, and he spoke slowly and distinctly like he was talking to a deaf child. "But ... you ... do ... not ... have ... a ... right ... to ... poison ... my ... son ... against ... his ... mother."

She took out her cell phone and started to make a call. "That won't help you here," Dad told her. "The cell tower is behind the hill." He pointed to the big hill to the west where she'd come up the road. "No one can hear you at all." He was acting weird and the woman looked a little nervous. I knew Dad was playacting because he talked that way sometimes when he played monster to get me to go to bed. "No one's going to come help you ..."

Then Dad turned to the officer, "Get this woman out of here before I do something we'll all regret." The woman was still fidgeting with her phone, but she was also edging toward the door as Dad said to her, "Take your hate ... and your fucking witch hunt ... somewhere else! Next time someone wants to talk with me, I want a lawyer, and send a real detective, not some bullshit Christian hate monger!"

The creek bed between us and Cy's place was usually pretty dry, but there were a few places that never totally dried out. Dad had an idea where to look for water because the rancher who'd sold my parents our house had taken everything except an abandoned photograph album I'd found while exploring in the back of a small closet.

A couple of pictures showed a pool by a hill with several adults and kids jumping in water that was up to their waist in some places. Dad recognized the shape of one of the large rocks, and we were able to find the rock by going to the dry creek bed and walking upstream or, more accurately, up where the water came from when it rained, for about twenty minutes. There were a few little puddles back deep under some of the trees away from the sun.

"There's probably just a trickle left from what used to be a real spring under there," Dad said. Then, of course, he had to explain to me what a spring was. "I bet there was water here most of the time before the drought."

Being smaller, I could easily get under the bush by the water. When I touched the water, it seemed to move like there was something in it.

Dad saw me jump back. "Here," he said. I'd not noticed, but he'd carried a jar along in his pocket. He pushed the low branches up so he could get to the puddle under the tree and dip the jar in to fill it. "We'll look at this at the house."

As we came in the back door, I tromped the dirt off my boots. Although I had no idea how to look into the water and see things, I told Mom, "Dad's got some water to look at." She looked up from her computer and smiled. I think she enjoyed how Dad got excited by unusual things.

Dad went to one of the bedrooms we never used and came back with a scratched wooden box that he set on the kitchen table. He opened the box. "This is a microscope." He turned his head and looked at the microscope from the side to be certain it was okay. "I used this in medical school." He added casually, "Your grandfather used it in medical school before that."

He never talked about my grandfather, and that was the first time I'd ever heard he'd gone to medical school. I eagerly waited for what he might say next, but Dad went on to handle the microscope. "You use this to look at things to make them bigger so you can seen them," he said, touching it like he was getting reacquainted with a friend he hadn't see for many years. He plugged in the cord and a light came on. He put a drop of the water from under the tree on a glass slide and peered into the scope. "Yes," he said with satisfaction. "Here, you look."

But I couldn't see a thing. He looked back into the scope himself, adjusted the focus, and had me look again. "You don't see the little organisms moving around?" he asked with frustration.

"No," I said. I was sorry to disappoint him.

He sat there for a moment. "Okay. Look again, and keep looking." All I could see was the light, and then for an instant a small thing wiggled in front of me, and then it was gone. "There," I said, excited to meet his expectation.

"You saw it?"

"Yes, but it went away."

"Let's try again." This time he turned the knob slower.

"There it is," I said, and this time the glimpse of movement lasted longer.

"Keep looking." He tuned the knob again. "Tell me when you keep seeing it." We kept this up until I could see the small organisms wiggling on the slide. But when it was set so I could see, Dad couldn't see.

He looked at me for a long time as though he was trying to understand something. Finally he said, "I think you need glasses. You see the stars, but not the microscope, at least not when it's set for me. Our eyes are different." He pondered out loud. "Huh?"

At the end of August, we went to Omaha to see an ophthalmologist just before Labor Day. Mom was a lot better, and she was back to doing some of the cooking. She would sit on a short stool and pull weeds in her herb garden, but she didn't run in the mornings like she used to. She came with us because she didn't want to stay home alone. Dad did all the driving, got the motel room for the night we were there, and set up the picnic lunch along the way.

We got up early to tend our two cows and leave feed for the chickens before we left. Cy would come over in the afternoon to check that everything was okay, but it wouldn't be polite to leave unnecessary work for him. Neighbors helped each other, but we kept our requests to a minimum. That was only fair.

My appointment was early the next morning, so we had an afternoon to go to the zoo and a movie theater. I'd never seen a giraffe or an elephant. A zebra at least made sense because it was like a horse and a few people around us had horses.

Mom explained where all the animals had lived in the past. "Most of the wild elephants were killed off in the bushmeat wars in Africa," she said. "The Asian ones did a bit better because a lot of people in India were already vegetarian." It was hard for me to follow a lot of what she said when she talked about areas as big as northern

Nebraska with elephants walking around in groups that no one owned. Dad listened as much as I did, and then said to me, "She's always loved animals, especially the big ones. That's how I could get her to live in the country."

"Yeah," she said. "Big promises, but there were hardly any left." I understood then that she had so many books of animal photographs because she'd never seen them in their wild homes.

The bright lights in the movie theater that night were overpowering. I was thrilled by commercial popcorn—by the whole concession stand. And the picture was unbelievable. At home we looked at movies on satellite TV, but here a face could look the size of the whole side of our house. The other treat in Omaha was ice cream. Neither Mom nor Dad ever bought ice cream because we lived so far from either Valentine or Chamberlain that it would melt before they got home.

It was hard to fall asleep that night.

In the morning, Mom got ready to go the doctor with us, but Dad knew she wanted to go the real library in Omaha and there might not be time after we left the doctor's office. "We'll be okay," he assured her. So we dropped her there on the way to my appointment.

Dr. Friend, the ophthalmologist, was a calm man

whose name fit him well. He and Dad greeted each other like old friends, and I learned on one of my follow-up visits that they had gone to school together. Dr. Friend asked why we were there, and since Dad had figured out what was not right, he did the talking. The doctor asked some general health questions. Dad answered.

Allergies?

"None."

Any medicines I took regularly?

"No."

Immunizations?

"They're current."

Did I exercise well?

"On a farm? You bet." He and my dad both chuckled.

Any other health issues?

"Mild hypospadias," Dad answered.

"Mild?" Dr. Friend asked.

"Yes," Dad answered. "Less than twenty percent. We decided it was better to keep it to ourselves to minimize any attention."

"Yeah. I understand completely. Well, your secret is safe with me, my friend."

At the end of his exam, Dr. Friend handed Dad a prescription for me to get glasses. "He probably doesn't need them for playing outside. He'll need them for classes," he said. Then he thought for a moment. "But he'll be doing the satellite classes, won't he? Well, they'll be useful for the computer and if he wants to look through your microscope again." Then he said to me, "Your dad's a great doctor. Remember that."

As we went out to the car to go pick Mom up at the library, I asked Dad, "What's hippo paid for us mean?"

"What?" He tried to understand.

I repeated myself, "Hippo paid for us? Like you told Dr. Friend."

"Oh, hypospadias. That means the opening on the end of your penis is a little longer than average."

I thought about this as we walked to the car. "What's a health issue?"

Dad could see where my questions were leading, but he had to concentrate on finding the library. "We'll talk about this later."

When he did, it was a short, doctor talk. "Girls have an open place between their legs," he began. "Boys don't. They have a penis. In the fetus, both boys and girls start with an opening. In boys, the opening is supposed to fold itself closed by about twelve weeks after the pregnancy starts. If it doesn't close right, the baby boy is born with an opening. The worse it is, the more he's like a girl."

He stopped as though he was ready for me to ask questions, but I was too confused to ask anything. He'd covered the biology in a sketchy way, but I had no idea how this would affect me.

I worried that I was supposed to do something about it or that I had caused a problem for my parents by being how I was. They were careful that I not see them without clothes, like there was a secret that they had. They both wore at least shorts, and my mother a shirt, when I was around. I peeked at my dad's medical books, but they were pretty clinical. In one of the older books there was a penis that was bigger than mine, and the hole came out the tip.

Of course I could look at myself, but once I was able to take my own bath, I was pretty much the only person who saw me. My dad didn't tell me too much other than to repeat that I had a small hypospadias. "It's probably easier if you don't let the other guys see you."

That was good advice, but I had to be humiliated to realize what good advice it had been.

We'd checked out of our motel first thing in the morning before we left Mom at the library, and the afternoon was on its way to being hot. On the way to get Mom, I noticed that the sign on the front of a bank already read 92° in the old Fahrenheit system. Mom was waiting on the curb as we approached. "Let's go to the Elmwood Pool," she said with more excitement than I'd seen in a while.

"Now? Before we drive home?" Dad asked.

"Sure. Jack's never been to a real pool. I haven't been there in years. It'll be fun."

But it wasn't.

We paid the admission and changed into shorts, but we didn't have real swimming suits, and the lifeguard told us we couldn't get in the water. Mom didn't argue about herself, but she tried to argue for me and Dad. It didn't work. The lifeguard pointed to the sign on the fence over the entry desk that read, "Proper Swim Wear Required."

Finally Mom said to the lifeguard, "Okay, if that's how it has to be. Where's a store around here?"

We got suits for Dad and me. Cheap ones from the sale rack because it was the end of the season. They were odd colors, but they were real swimsuits.

There were no women's suits on sale so Mom didn't get one. She said it wasn't worth it to use just one time. But she was wearing long pants, and the lifeguard still wouldn't let her come in the pool area with us. That was unfair, because it had been her idea and she was the one who was excited because she remembered the name of the pool. We pretended to have fun while she watched us. She wanted it that way, but it wasn't fun without her. I'd never been in a pool, and I splashed around and coughed on water in my throat when Dad tried to teach me to swim. He swam pretty well. In the early evening, we got dressed and drove home.

I'd seen motorcycles on the highway before, sometimes in groups of two or three, but going home that night, there were huge groups. I counted more than forty in one group alone. They would come up behind us and cruise there for awhile. Then the lead cycle would pull up parallel to Dad for a moment, rev up and charge ahead.

I don't think they were trying to tell Dad to let them pass, but he eased off the accelerator when we were swarmed by a mob of bikers. Most of the men wore leather jackets, a lot of them with metal studs. About half had long hair billowing behind them, and some had a woman hanging on behind.

None of them wore helmets. They had mirrored sunglasses so you couldn't see where they were looking or guess what they were thinking. We were in their way, but they didn't bother with us.

"Who are they?" I asked. "Probably guys going to Sturgis," Dad answered. He explained the huge bike rally that had gone on in South Dakota every August for as long as anyone could remember. "They'll probably keep riding all night to get there."

Dad told me that Sturgis was on the east side of the Black Hills, and the Black Hills had been thought so useless that the Lakota were forced to live there until someone discovered gold. Then the Lakota were offered other land that they did not accept until they had lost several more big battles with the U.S. government. After that, they were forced to settle in what became the Pine Ridge Reservation. Dad had heard these stories from the Lakota perspective when he was in the Indian Health Service. He believed the Lakota version because the government's version was based on someone getting rich from the gold mines.

There were a lot fewer bikes when we turned off Route 20 for the last hour home. That night, however, we heard one group drive nearby on the road west of our home. Sound travels on a cool night, and when you have that many motorcycles, they make a lot of noise.

I had the impression that Dad was excited to hear the noise in the distance. He never rode a motorcycle that I knew, but he always listened hard when he heard one.

It took all summer for Mom to get better. She lay in bed a lot, listening to old music that she said her mother liked. I don't know if she'd heard Dad yell at the woman and the officer. She might have been sleeping. And try as I could, I couldn't figure out what she'd done that made it so I'd never have a little brother.

A few hours every day she'd come down to the kitchen and work with me on learning simple things, starting with the alphabet and moving on to beginning reading and simple arithmetic.

In September, she signed me up for satellite school. Before the Big Drought, there had been enough kids to need a school. Now the building was still there, but it was only used a little bit. The state matched the U.S. government putting money into a system of lessons that kids watched on their home computers every morning, Monday through Friday. I watched in the kitchen and Mom sat beside me during the lessons.

Every kid's computer had a built-in camera, and on the computer screen I saw the teacher and a row of pictures of the other kids in my session. There were usually thirty or so kids' faces. Most lived many miles away, but for satellite school, it didn't matter where you lived.

The first and third Mondays, Tuesdays and Wednesdays of every month, Mom drove me to the school where I'd sit in a class with other kids who were within a year or two of my age, older or younger. A teacher, Mr. Martin, drove up from Omaha and taught things like history and social studies that weren't specific to one age or another and, unlike arithmetic, could be taught in any order. Thursdays and Fridays, the days after he taught us, he went to a similar school in another really rural area, about fifty miles away. The weeks between he was somewhere else.

They used three rooms in the building, one for young kids, one for older kids, and one for those in between.

Every fall, they reassigned groups to keep us with kids roughly our age, but basically there were three groups at all times. There was always a parent in the class with Mr. Martin so he could go from one to another of the three rooms, and so the kids were never left alone. Ronnie was the only kid I knew in person when I started school, except I'd kind of met some of the other kids through their pictures during computer classes. Those days in class were the only time the other kids and I were together face to face.

At Halloween, the satellite schoolteacher had everyone make a mask and wear it, so their faces didn't show. Then she scrambled the pictures around on the screen, and we played a game, voting on our electronic response pads to try to figure out who each person was behind his or her mask. About half the class guessed me right on the first try. I started right away planning how to disguise myself better the next year, but the teacher changed and the new teacher didn't like that game.

Mom had planned to be a teacher before she met Dad, but she told me that getting married to Dad ended that dream. Now that I'm older I think it would be more accurate to say it was getting pregnant with me that ended her dream. She loved the days that she was the parent in class with Mr. Martin. She smiled the days she had to leave me off by myself because another parent was on duty in the class, but I could tell she wished she could go in with me. When I got in the car to go home, she always asked the same question. "Where did you travel today?"

It was important for her to dream of travel. When we had a class on England, she got very excited. "I was an exchange student to England during college. We went into London several times. I have some pictures I took. I'll show you when we get home. It was before the floods covered the old Parliament buildings ... such a beautiful place." Then she repeated to herself, "... before the floods."

I'd heard of the time before the floods, when a dike and a sea gate kept the ocean out of London, but school didn't say much about it, and neither did Mom. No one wanted to remember that. Maybe that's why she never got around to showing me the pictures.

Dad got a few emergency calls in the night. Most of them were from women starting to have their babies. We had electric power, with a backup solar panel for electronic stuff, but we didn't have a phone into the farm that worked off a wire. As Dad told the woman who asked the questions about Mom, the cell tower was over the top of the hill, so it worked well on the highway but not at our place.

When someone needed to call Dad, they called the

regional emergency call center, which was actually in Omaha. The operator would take down the details, and then call Dad on his satellite phone. That was always on in the kitchen. I wasn't allowed to use it except the one time to call 9-1-1 for Mom, but that was only because Dad had told me to do it.

I always knew when he left on a call at night. He tried to be quiet, and I think Mom was used to it so she went back to sleep. But I would lie there and wonder where he had gone.

One very cold night, there was even a little snow on the ground, I heard the rumble of a motorcycle coming up the road toward our house. I went to my bedroom window. There was no moon, and the only place I could see anything was by the barn, where the yard light was on. Dad didn't like to contribute to what he called "light pollution," so we had just that one small light in case there was trouble with the animals.

As the motorcycle got closer, I could see its headlight sweeping slowly as the rider worked his way around the turns coming into our yard. Then I heard our door open and Dad stepped out. He waited to approach until the rider had cut the engine. Unlike the riders going to Sturgis, this man wore a helmet, and when he took it off, I saw that he had long white hair. He was tall, and very thin, and my reaction was to wonder how such a thin man could control such a powerful bike.

Dad stepped out and gave the rider a big hug. They stood there for a long time, two men hugging each other, long enough that I was puzzled and embarrassed to be watching. Then they walked over to the barn and sat out of the wind by the door. As I watched them, I fell back asleep.

I don't know how long they talked, but I was awakened again by the noise when the motorcycle started up and the rider revved the engine a few times. Dad stood and watched as the rider balanced the cycle between his legs, walking it into a turn toward our driveway. Dad called to him. I could not make out the words, but he walked over to the man who was still astride the idling bike and hugged him again.

Dad came in the house and turned off the yard light, which he'd never done in my memory. I couldn't see anything at first, but as my eyes adjusted to the darkness, I could make out shadows of the barn in the starlight.

When I came downstairs in the morning, I heard Mom and Dad talking in the kitchen. They weren't arguing, but I heard Mom say to Dad, "There's something wrong about this." I paused around the corner from the kitchen. "Normal people live in a house, or at least an apartment. You really don't have any idea where he lives or anything?" she asked.

"Nope."

"It's weird," she said. "Kind of makes you wonder

what he's up to. What's he live on anyway?"

"He probably has savings of some kind. I have no idea," Dad replied. "He used to keep up his medical license with a post office box, but he let that go a couple of years ago. I'm in the dark as much as you are. Sometimes I think he's still getting over Mom."

"That was six years ago," she said.

"Yeah, but there was something about her and his bike. You saw the way he rode off after the funeral ..." I shifted my foot, the floor squeaked, and they stopped talking. "That you, Jack?" Mom called out.

I came around the corner. "Hi, Mom," I said. Dad didn't look at me as he poured a cup of coffee.

"So, Jack," said Mom in an overly cheerful voice. "What do you want for breakfast?"

Dad was already out of the room.

In the spring, Cy bought an old bull and offered to "service" Dad's two cows. No one explained to me what service meant, but I gathered that it had something to do with a cow, what my dad called a heifer, having a calf in the winter. We'd never had any calves, and when Dad started talking about servicing the cows, Mom asked him if he thought there would be enough water for the cows to be healthy, along with a calf. "I just don't want to get attached to a lot of animals and then watch them die." Dad said he had a plan, so she agreed he could go ahead.

On the first Saturday in June, I helped Dad load our two cows up the ramp into the back of our trailer. He tried to explain that it meant something when one cow got on top of another, and I smiled and nodded, but as I've learned several times over, the details don't mean a thing until you know the plan.

Ronnie and his dad got to Cy's before we arrived. They didn't bring any cows, but they wanted to watch. Doc Porter was there, too.

Dad led both of our cows out of the trailer and into a pen. He slipped a halter onto the head of one and pulled the rope around a big post while he stroked the cow's head and spoke softly into its ear. Doc Porter looked at both cows and said, "I think you're right on this one, but the other I'm not sure. Won't hurt, but don't have any big expectations."

Cy brought his bull into the pen and let it smell the back of the cow. I was watching from the end of the cow where its head was. Suddenly, the bull jumped up on the back of the cow with his front legs one on each side of the cow, and a long pink shiny thing came down between its legs. I would have thought it was a penis like a boy or a man had, but it hadn't been there and it suddenly appeared and stuck out.

Then, almost as quickly, the bull dropped back and off the cow, and I caught just a glimpse of the pink part sliding back up between the bull's legs. Dad was surprised it happened so fast. "That's it?" he asked Cy and Doc Porter.

"Yep," Cy said. "Now you see why you city folks might miss it. Sort of like a teenager trying out a new toy. Always in a hurry." The men laughed.

We had lunch to allow time for the bull to rest before they did the same thing with our other cow. As we sat there, Cy asked Dad, "Did you tell Jack here about our company this summer?"

"No. I didn't get around to it. You tell him." I paid attention, since we rarely had anyone new in our area. Mom said we couldn't call it a neighborhood since we all lived too far apart.

"Our granddaughter is going to spend the summer with us after her school is out."

"Oh," was all I could muster.

"Oh?" my dad asked. "Is that all you can say?"

Cy saved me. "Don't worry, Percy. They'll either get along or not."

But I asked one question, "What's her name?"

"Millie," Cy said with a smile.

After lunch, the men decided they'd waited long enough. They tied the second cow to the same post and brought in the bull again. Afterwards, as we loaded our cows into the trailer, Doc Porter slapped the rump of the second one just before Dad lifted the tailgate. "We'll see how it goes."

Two weeks later, Dad and I walked over to Cy's to work his calves for the year. Ronnie's dad also had two more calves. As we got ready to start, Dad asked Cy, "Do you think it would be good to keep the two bulls this year? Your bull is getting a little older. Maybe have a backup bull in a year or so."

"Hmmm. Not a bad idea," Cy said. They gave all the calves their shots, but keeping the bulls meant there weren't any oysters.

About six weeks later, Doc Porter came by our place and said that one cow was with calf but the second one wasn't. Dad thought about putting the second cow with the bull again, but he never got around to it.

We usually lived on the water from the well, but as Mom had said, we couldn't draw enough water to care for a cow that was going to have a calf. We'd hoped to have two cows with two calves, but we still needed to double our water even for the two cows and one calf. Dad's idea was to build a small earth dam to catch water in the dry creek bed when it rained. That would not last all year, but while we used that water, we could stop pumping water from our well for the cows and the chickens. He hired Jonathan, a friend of Cy's who owned a bulldozer.

Jonathan showed up early on a Saturday morning. It was important that he get in and out on the weekend, so he arrived just at sunup. He and Dad maneuvered his trailer to a place near the creek bed, to the left as you walked to Cy's, and the opposite way from the pool where we'd got the water to look at with a microscope.

There were two trees there that seemed to get by on no water at all. "I figure there's a bit of moisture under there all the time," Dad explained. "We can put the dam so it blends in with the trees."

"Kind of an underground stream?" asked Jonathan. Dad nodded. So Jonathan set to work and pushed dirt and rock to build a pile that would be a dam when it rained. "Just hope the water folks in Sioux City don't see this," he said as he loaded the dozer onto the trailer late in the afternoon.

"I doubt they'll miss my little bit," said Dad. "You can't see this from the road, and they won't have any reason to come over the hill to look. I think it'll be okay. I'll add some scrub brush and taper the middle to look the same." Some of the freshly moved dirt looked darker where it had been moist under the ground. "This'll all dry out by Monday. They won't look on the weekend."

"Yep." Jonathan laughed. "Government employees." He waved as he put his truck in gear and edged up the bank to leave. "Good luck, Doc."

Cy called on July 1 when his granddaughter arrived for the summer. I had walked to his place so many times with my dad, my parents thought it was okay for me to walk over by myself. The only rule was to ask Cy to make a short call on Dad's emergency phone when I got there and again when I was leaving to come back.

Millie was about the same height as me and about the same size. I was pretty tall for the boys in my class, and taller than the girls my age, so I assumed she was a lot older than me. But we sorted that out in our first conversation when she asked how old I was.

"I'll be seven August 28," I said.

"I won't be seven until September."

That surprised me, and it also surprised me that although Cy and Martha were her grandparents, she'd never been to their farm just half a day up from Omaha. She had never been around a cow or a chicken, and she had no sense of the dust and random bushes and scrub brush on a ranch.

But other things came up when Millie talked about her parents. "My dad travels almost all the time. He always brings me a little present from wherever he's been. I have a lot of little bells and statues from Chicago and Albany and places."

"Have you ever been there?"

"No, but Dad says he'll take me when I'm older."

"The biggest place I've ever been is Omaha."

"Omaha is such a dump. That's what Mom says. She says she'd never have gone there with my dad if she thought she'd be there ten years later. Funny, I'd think that growing up out here with Cy and Martha ..." Millie called her grandparents by their first names, "... she'd have thought Omaha was heaven."

I had nothing to say back or share about my parents. Mom and Dad were so predictable that talking about them was boring. That made me boring, too.

"I think the reason she says that is she took a trip to New York before she met Dad," Millie continued, "and before the sea wall broke in the hurricane, whenever that was. It was some kind of school trip with a lot of girls. There were adults to watch them, but she and some friends snuck off. Dad yelled at her about that one time, and she just told him to fuck himself."

Millie didn't care what kind of words she used. I didn't say a thing because Mom and Dad would never talk that way, and I couldn't think of any words that wouldn't make me sound more stupid.

"She still has a couple of postcards from that trip, and sometimes she just sits and looks at them. It's like she blames Dad for the flood or something."

Millie abruptly changed the conversation, "So what do you do for the Fourth of July?"

"We usually go to Valentine if the weather's okay."

The next day, Cy dropped Millie off at our house. Mom was very friendly and made us sandwiches. After lunch, I took Millie upstairs to show her my room. She pointed to the bathroom door and asked, "What's that?"

When I showed her how it went through to the other bedroom and into the hall, she started looking around more, and she made me see our house through her surprised eyes. Mom and Dad and I used the two bedrooms and the two bathrooms, and since they were right at the top of the stairs, we stopped thinking about the whole rest of the second floor, the four other bedrooms and three baths that were never used because we never had guests who stayed overnight.

Millie walked down the hall opening the door to each room. There were boxes piled and spread out in two rooms, but the other two were as empty as the day we moved in. As she moved on, Millie spent more time looking at each room, until she just gazed around and around the last one. "You live in a palace," she said.

Cy drove Millie to our house so she could go to Valentine with us, but there was a massive storm just west of us. It was so close to our home that Valentine didn't get even a drop of rain, but for miles around us, power was out two nights and a day. There were tornado warnings, and one touched down about an hour away. No one was killed, but it was a big deal and one family lost their home.

Dad said that was why the rancher had built our house on the east side of a tall hill. “Big storms almost always move from west to east in this area,” he explained to Millie and me. “Because he put the house on the east side, the hill protects us from any big damage. It’s like a wall between us and almost any storm.”

When it came time for Millie to go home, Dad walked with us to the creek bed to be sure the water had gone back down enough that it was safe to wade across. The storm had ended a couple hours earlier, and the ground was so dry that the water soaked in or ran off almost immediately.

When we got to the creek, he walked downstream to check the dam and the new water pond. Sure enough, it held a lot of water, not deep, but perhaps fifty yards or so back from the dam. “Perfect,” Dad said.

The water was low enough in the creek itself that we could walk over to Cy’s, but it was too late to go to Valentine. We didn’t have any fireworks, but Cy got out his shotgun and fired into the air. “Probably more authentic for what the patriots shot off anyway,” he commented.

Then he let Millie fire both barrels into the air, and me, too.

The next day, Dad dropped me at Cy's place on his way to make a house call. Millie and I played around, and then I remembered the picture we'd found in our house with the people by the pool in the creek bed. I told Millie about the picture and wondered out loud what the rain had done. "Maybe the pool is full of water. Do you want to see?"

I wasn't usually that daring, to do things without asking my mom or my dad, but she started toward the path as soon as I mentioned the idea and before I had a chance to second-guess myself.

The path was still a bit muddy in the shady places as we went down to the creek, but it didn't take long. The creek bed was down to a trickle so I assumed the pool would be nearly dry, but it wasn't. Water remained over an area about thirty feet wide. I took off my shoes and waded in up to my knees, but I was only a little way from the bank.

"Let's swim," Millie said. I still felt the embarrassment of trying to swim at the pool in Omaha, so I made an excuse. "We don't have swimming suits, not even pretend ones."

"We can swim in our underwear," she said, and she took off her T-shirt and shorts. I followed her lead, and we both waded into the water in our underpants. From the bank we looked much the same except her hair was longer and pulled back in an elastic. Our flat bare chests were the same. Millie's underpants stuck to the crease on her bottom, and I assume mine stuck to me the same way. The only difference was that her underpants were smooth in front, and mine had the bump from my deformed hypospadias penis. I didn't want her to notice, so I kept holding one hand or the other over myself, even as I ran. Millie, however, ran gracefully, swinging both arms widely, as if her arms helped move her body through the air.

Then she saw the rock I'd told her about in the photograph and climbed up on it. "Watch me," she said and jumped.

The water dragged her underpants down slightly as she stood up, and I stood mesmerized to see even a little of the secret parts of another person's body. The older me would call that a sexual observation, but at that age, I was fascinated to see that someone else looked so much like me except for the difference in just one place.

After she called me chicken, I climbed on the rock and jumped in, too. Then we lay in the sun until our underwear dried and we put back on our shorts and shoes. I walked with her to the top of the hill that overlooked Cy's place and waited while she walked down to the farmyard.

She waved from the door before I walked home. I was happy to have a friend.

The rest of the summer passed quickly. With Dad's permission, I used his microscope to show her the little organisms in the water from the pool in the creek. Millie stayed at our place late one night and Dad took us both out to show her the Milky Way before he drove her home. Because of the light pollution, you could never see that from Omaha. She spent one night in the bedroom that shared my bathroom, and Dad made us pancakes in the morning. He liked to pour shapes as he cooked. He poured an "M" pancake for Millie, and a "J" one for me.

Then it was September. I walked over to Cy's to say good-bye before Millie went back to Omaha. "Jack ..." she said before she closed the car door and rolled down the window. "See you next summer." It would be a long time not to have a friend.

Dad hadn't been a member of the Boy Scouts, but he told me about them and said some of his friends had been in a troop when he was growing up. Among the boys my age who might have been in Scouts, everyone lived too far apart to have any kind of regular meeting. You didn't waste gas going to meetings unless they were important, like school, and the idea of taking tests to prove you had learned certain survival skills was a joke.

Surviving in north central Nebraska was its own merit badge.

We did, however, have deer season.

Dad said it was a tribute to Mother Nature's ingenuity that any deer survived in our area. But they did, and in the fall dads went on a weekend camping trip with their sons. The men without sons came along to swell the crowd and increase the camaraderie, and the men with daughters left them at home. This was a male adventure.

Each year a different site was selected for camping, but the sites were always within and hour or two of home. Dad had a shotgun to keep foxes from our chickens, but he didn't own the kind of rifle the men used to hunt. We were always invited, however, because all the men knew Dad was who they'd call if they needed help right away.

In the evenings, the dads sat around in camp and told stories. I think there would have been a campfire, except there were so few trees that it would have been very dim. Instead, one of the dads had a bunch of light bulbs that he ran on a series of old car batteries. He had them charged when we arrived on Friday night and used a salvaged solar panel to recharge them in the daylight on Saturday.

We got to sleep after midnight on Friday night, and everyone slept too late to get up early enough to hunt the first full day. They didn't talk about it, but it was pretty clear that several of the dads had spiked their soda pop with alcohol. One dad went berserk when his son picked up his soda pop and got ready to take a sip.

Because everyone had overslept so much, there wasn't any cause for new bragging from the morning hunt, so we were all kind of bored. Our campsite was on one of the few creeks that flowed year round, probably fed by a lot of small springs that had survived the drought. So the kids went wading and played around the creek while the dads told stories and bragged about exaggerated hunts in the past.

It was cold, and I didn't want to get in the water, but there was a low tree branch that extended over the creek about six or eight feet out from the bank, just a foot or so above the water. I sat on that and edged out closer to the place where the more daring boys had gotten into the creek itself.

Ronnie was there. He talked to me like usual, but he was trying to be friends with a guy named Charles. Charles was a couple years older and lived over an hour away, so I'd never had a conversation with him.

Charles saw vulnerability in my desire to stay out of the water, and he immediately stood on the bank of the creek, put his foot on the branch I was sitting on, and started to kick it down to shake me off. I was looking the other way, and as I tried to maintain my grip, I lost my balance and fell in.

"Oops," said Charles.

"Bastard," I mumbled, but not too loud because although I was tall for my age, he outweighed me by at least twenty pounds.

He heard me. "Hey, Kobb. What'd you say?"

"Nothing." I regretted being on the camping trip, I regretted going on the branch, and I regretted even trying to pretend defiance.

"No! You said something," he insisted.

"Nothing," I repeated.

He grabbed my collar but avoided getting wet by not actually grabbing my body. "Bitch," he called me. "Come on bitch." He pushed me, and I stumbled backwards. "Let him go, Charles," Ronnie tried to intervene.

"No." Charles grabbed at me again. "I don't like this little wise ass." He was big enough to push me wherever he wanted to, so he grabbed my shoulder with one hand and my crotch with the other. Then he squeezed my crotch and my penis 'til it hurt. But he paused in surprise and looked me straight in the eye, "What the fuck kind of freak are you?"

My imagination jumped to my hypospadias. That had to be it, but I didn't pause to question how he could have felt that through my pants as he goosed me to show how he could humiliate me. While he hesitated deciding what to do next, I broke free and ran back to the dads.

I was safe there. As I said, no matter what they might

have felt in private, the men knew it was Dad who'd care for them after a moment of misjudgment or simply the bad luck that caused so many accidents. And Charles was subdued as soon as he realized he couldn't explain what he'd felt. He just yelled after me, "You're a freak. That's what you are. You're a freak."

I sat in my dad's truck. It was cold outside, but the sky was clear, so the cab got warm like any room on a sunny afternoon. My dad waited until the center of attention had moved on, and then he came over to the truck and asked if I was okay. "Yeah," I felt I had to reassure him. "I'll be all right." Then it all got the better of me. "It's just that he hurt me and then called me names." I was starting to cry. "I didn't do anything to him."

"I know," said my dad. "I don't know why some folks are like that."

A few dads went out to hunt in the late afternoon when the deer were browsing just before it got dark. Some guns were fired, but no deer were hit. It was like Charles's yelling had changed something in the air that could not be undone.

No one stayed up late, so some of the dads got up before sunup Sunday, and that time one deer was killed. The person who got the deer was Cy, which seemed fitting because he was the most senior person on the trip.

It was snowing when I went to bed about a week after New Years, and I couldn't sleep. Dad was acting strange, and I didn't know if he was upset and, if he was, why. An hour or so after I turned out the light, I heard a motorcycle that sounded like the one I'd seen when Dad talked to the rider last year. When I peeked out the window, it was the same man, and again, Dad greeted him with a hug. They talked for a few minutes, but this time, instead of going to the barn to talk, they put the man's motorcycle in the barn and walked into the house together.

They were really quiet. I couldn't hear even a mumble from what they were saying, if they were talking at all. I kept straining my ears and peeked again at the accumulating snow before I fell asleep.

In the morning, I woke up when my dad slammed the door from the mudroom to the yard. I watched him walk through a foot of fresh snow to the barn, and it seemed like any other winter morning as he pulled out some seed for the chickens. I couldn't see if the motorcycle was still there, but when I got out of bed, I realized that my door to the bathroom was closed.

When I went into the upstairs hall, I smelled bacon. That didn't make sense because this wasn't a weekend. In the kitchen, the gray haired man was busy at the stove.

"Hi, Jack," he said when he saw me. "I'm Kobb." He held out his hand.

"I'm Kobb," I replied. "Jack Kobb."

"Yeah, I know that. I'm Perseus Kobb, but I go by Kobb."

"My dad's Perseus Kobb," I protested.

"Well, technically, he's Perseus Kobb *Junior*." The man smiled as though he was letting me in on a great joke. "He's named after me. His mom wanted that. And he sure wasn't named before me."

I sat at the table. He handed me a plate with two pancakes shaped like a "J" and a "K." "You make pancakes like my dad does," I said.

"Nope," he corrected me. "Your dad makes pancakes like I showed him."

I heard Dad stomping his boots free of snow in the mudroom. "I see you two've met," he said as he came through the inner door into the kitchen. "This is your grandfather. Everyone calls him Kobb."

Logically, I needed a grandfather somewhere, but I wouldn't have picked this skinny old man with a silver ponytail, and a beard that grew down on his neck and stuck out in many directions. He seemed out of place on the ranch or farm or however you'd classify our home, and he seemed out of place in my life.

Mom joined us, and we all chatted about nothing I

can remember as we ate. Then Dad had to make a house call on one of his patients who'd refused a flu vaccine in the fall and now had the flu. The new antivirus medications would help, but Dad always got upset that someone's refusal to take simple precautions made him use a valuable drug unnecessarily. "I'm the custodian of these medicines," was his usual comment. "When I was young, we went through a time when the old drugs stopped working, and we had to do our best until the new drugs were discovered.

"It's so unnecessary. So unnecessary ..."

"I remember those days," Kobb added. "It was hell. I had patients dying from stupid things, yeah, stupid things like the flu." He turned to me to change the subject. "Did your dad tell you I named you? 'Jack' was my idea."

"No," I replied, and then to answer a burning question of my own, "Why'd you call me Jack?"

"I knew someone named Jack once, a very brave man. He'd do anything for you." He tried to be casual, but his expression was like he'd stumbled on a rock and barely kept himself from falling. "He died a long time ago."

"What happened to him?" I asked.

"That's a long story. Some other time."

Mom watched the two of us until she was sure that part of the conversation had ended, because although I don't think she knew much, she must have known how important the guy named Jack was to Kobb. Then she got up and carried our dishes to the sink.

"You better help your mom," Kobb said over his shoulder as he walked into the living room.

Cy called just past noon. He had not expected the snow to be so bad, and he'd left his bull out in pasture. This morning it was limping severely.

Kobb, Dad, and I rode over in Dad's pick up. Doc Porter was helping someone with a breech calf on a heifer that had gotten pregnant out of planned season, so Dad examined the bull. "I'd wait until Doc Porter checks him out, but I think he's hurt his forefoot. Might be broken," Dad said.

Doc Porter confirmed a broken bone a few hours later, and his next words were pretty grim. "There's no real way to help him. You can't cast it like a person's foot. He'd just kick until he kicked it off. The vets down in Omaha could put a rod down the middle of the bone, but we'd have to get him down there, it'd be real expensive for them to do it, and even then, he's so big I wouldn't expect it to hold up very long."

We all stood around and didn't say much for a while. Then Kobb spoke up and said what everyone didn't want to think, "Hell. There's a lot of beef there that we shouldn't really just put in the ground as a carcass. He was good a couple of hours ago. The meat will be tough as hell, but it'd be crazy to waste it. It'll be okay as stew or hamburger."

So it was decided that the bull would be put down and we'd salvage what meat we could. Doc Porter was a vet, so he could check the bull's health internally before we used the beef, but it still felt weird to be using a bull for meat. It was bad luck that the bull had hurt himself, but none of us had resources to waste. I looked away when the Doc stunned the bull, and they used a pulley and Dad's truck to lift him up. "I guess it was good foresight to keep those two bulls," Cy said. "At least we have a backup plan."

Kobb stayed with us for a week. I called him granddad one time, and he corrected me. "My friends call me Kobb. I'm not old enough to be a granddad." And that was that.

He was hard to figure sometimes. For example, after the first morning when he was trying not to wake me up, he never shut his door to the bathroom. It didn't bother him that I kept my door closed, but his was usually open. It made me wonder what he was used to, where did he usually live, but I never asked.

Like most guys my age, I sat to use the toilet, even to pee. I knew that Dad could stand behind a tree, but even when we were on the farm but away from the house, I'd always pull down my pants and squat. I don't know why I started that. Maybe it was at school, because in the schoolhouse, there weren't what I've learned used to be called urinals in the boys' bathroom. You could see places where there were newer tiles in the floor like something had been there and was gone. So like all the other boys, I sat to use the toilet.

The night before he left, I was sitting on the toilet when Kobb said from the other room, "You can stand up to pee. Did you know that? It'll work for you." He wasn't watching me, or anything weird, but the door was open and he knew I heard him.

"What?" I asked.

"I said," he explained, "your friends need to sit so they don't make a mess. They don't have enough down there to make it point anywhere else. But you really don't need to sit." He still didn't come in, but he continued, "Try it, standing up, it's easier and quicker. Here, I'll leave you alone." He shut his door.

I stood in there by myself, and lowered my underwear before I tried to pee standing up. Kobb was right. The hypospadias made the stream point down a little bit, but if I stood over the toilet, I didn't need to sit.

But it felt awkward to have Kobb telling me this, and on top of that, I couldn't understand how he knew what I could do. I went back to my room. There were big things that I didn't understand, probably things that Kobb shared with my dad, but this time I didn't close my door.

After a few minutes, Kobb used the toilet, and then he stood at the open door to my room. "I wish you could've known Jack."

"Jack?"

"The Jack you're named after."

I was already bothered that someone I hardly knew was talking about my life before I could remember. It was my life, not his, and besides, all I had was my dad's word that this man was my grandfather. "Who was Jack?" I asked.

"Jack," said Kobb, and then he paused. "Jack was a guy I used to know. Jack was gone before your dad was born. Great guy. He'd do anything for you, Jack." Kobb had lost his focus and called me by the name he said he'd given me, but I wasn't certain which Jack he thought he was speaking to, me or the other one who'd died years ago. As though he was talking to a person I couldn't see, he repeated, "… anything."

Without another word, Kobb turned and went to his room. But as he was about to turn off the bathroom light he looked at me and had a smile on his face. I think he was happy with me.

It didn't stay cold in the winter anymore and the dam at the creek caught a lot of snowmelt as it warmed up. We stopped using the pump to water the cows well into March. Meanwhile, Dad watched the belly of the pregnant cow and listened to the calf's heart with his stethoscope. He had me listen, too. We'd been around her a lot over the years, so she tolerated us.

He'd been counting days from her breeding with the bull—when she was serviced—and brought her into the fenced area by the barn about three weeks before she was due. "Cow's pregnancy is about like a woman's," he told me. "Nine months plus or minus a few days. "

Her udder got really big and swollen, and then one morning she started bellowing. Dad called Doc Porter and then told me to come with him and watch. He showed me how the folds of skin below what he called the cow's anus were pink and swollen. She leaked some bloody liquid and kept bellowing. Sometimes she'd lie down. After awhile she'd raise her body on her forelegs and stand up. She went back and forth. Doc Porter arrived about the time the first hoof appeared from her vagina. Almost immediately, there was a pair of hooves.

Doc Porter soothed her while she continued to move around as though trying to find a position that didn't hurt. She'd stand and circle, lie down, and then stand again. All the time she made enough noise so that Mom came out from the house to watch, too.

Slowly the cow's grunts and bellowing began to push the hooves out, and finally the calf's nose. The cow circled and fidgeted, but nothing else happened. This continued for over an hour with the cow circling and the hooves and the calf's nose sticking out behind. "She needs help," Doc said.

He went to the back of his car and returned with a long pole with a half circle of rods set crosswise at one end. He got behind the cow and attached two ropes to the calf's hooves. Then he positioned the rods to hold the end of the pole stable against the back of the cow. I was puzzled because now the cow had a long pole attached behind it.

But I hadn't noticed that the rope loops were attached to the pole, and once everything was in place, Doc worked a ratchet on the pole and began to pull the calf out of the cow by tightening the ropes. As the calf's whole head appeared, it began to breathe. The cow was tired, but she grunted instinctively. The shoulders slipped out in a jerk. Doc cranked more, and the hips and finally the legs started out.

"Help catch it," he ordered Dad and me. So Dad and I held the calf from opposite sides. I felt the wet warmth of the newborn calf as its fluid smeared my shirt and jeans and we lowered it to the hay on the floor.

I was mesmerized by the calf's labored breathing. The cow stopped bellowing and turned to nuzzle the calf and start licking it dry. The calf lay on its side like it, too, had to rest from the ordeal. Then it lifted its head toward the cow and stood up.

Our new calf was a heifer, so all she needed was her shots. Cy's cows had had two males and Ronnie's dad's one, so we all brought our calves together for Doc Porter to work the calves at Cy's place. After he'd given them their shots and worked the male calves, Doc put the oysters aside to get down to the business of having the bulls from last year service the cows that had freshened. That was one of our two cows and one of Cy's cows.

Like last year, he tethered the first cow to the post. The young bull was brought in. He sniffed the cow, but he didn't have a good idea what to do. After some waiting, Dad pulled the bull toward the back of the cow while Cy and Ronnie's dad kept the bull centered on her back until he finally got up on her like the old bull had. Everyone was relieved until they realized there was no pink thing coming out toward the cow.

The bull curled the underside of his body toward the cow like he was supposed to, but nothing happened. Then a bunch of white stuff started dripping out where we'd been expecting his penis. We all were silent until Dad spoke, "Oh, god! It's gotten to the cattle, too." He put on a doctor glove and reached under the young bull to scrape up as much of the white stuff as he could. He sniffed it and said to me in a voice I'd never heard from him, full of near panic. "Jack, go tell Martha to run a pan on the stove, an empty pan, until it gets hot. Then bring me the pan and two eggs. Don't boil anything in the pan. Just get it real hot, but empty. Now hurry!"

It took about ten minutes to heat a pan, and then run back with it and two eggs. Dad had gotten a mess of the white stuff in his gloved hand and held his fingers curled around his palm so it wouldn't dry. "Put the pan on the table," he directed. "Did it cool enough to touch on the way down here?"

I touched the pan with a quick tap; it had cooled in the air as I brought it to the pen. "It's cool, Dad."

"Cy, crack the eggs into the pan. Keep it as clean as you can." When Cy had done this, Dad put his gloved hand into the eggs and massaged the white stuff into the egg, yolk and all. When his glove only showed mixed up eggs, he took a breath, slipped off the gloves, and laid the paper package they came in across the top of the pan. He turned to Doc Porter who seemed to understand what Dad meant, "Do you think we can make this work?"

"We won't lose anything by trying." So Dad and Cy got the other young bull, and I got another hot pan and two more eggs. This time they washed the bottom of the bull's stomach, and like the first one, when the second bull got on top of the cow, there was just dripping white stuff.

"I saw a YouTube of this one time," Dad said, "but it looked a whole lot easier with their equipment." They got the cow between steel sections of fence, they squeezed in the sides, and Dad got behind her. His glove only covered his hand, but he wasn't in a mood to lose time. Dad reached into the cow's back end like where a calf would come out and felt around. "Got the syringe?" he asked Doc. "You want to do this? You're the vet."

"Here." Doc Porter filled a syringe with the egg stuff and handed it to Dad. "I've never done it either, and you're doing what I'd do if it was me."

Dad took as much of the egg and white stuff as he could into the syringe and reached into the cow's backside again. "Here goes," he said. When he took his handout a few moments later, the syringe was empty.

Doc Martin did the next cow. When they'd been released, we all sat down and said nothing for a long time.

"Do you think you can drug one of the bulls asleep?" Dad asked Doc Porter.

"I guess so. I use ketamine for cows in labor if I need to. Should work for a bull, too."

The next day, Doc Porter gave one of the bulls a big dose of ketamine. We watched as the bull staggered, then lay down with its eyes open like it was looking at us.

Dad sloshed disinfectant on the bull's stomach and used a doctor scissor to cut back the skin where we'd expected the bull's penis to stick out.

There was a lot of bleeding, but Dad brought some suture from his doctor bag and over-sewed the edges as he went. Finally he got to what looked like I expected the pink part to look like, but it was very small. "I think we ought to leave this open," he said to Cy since it was his bull. "It'll make it easier to collect semen. We can clean it better."

Dad followed news on his computer as long as I could remember, but now he got on his computer to study raising cattle almost any time he wasn't making a house call or answering some person's call for medical advice. He looked at a lot of videos about breeding cows. He found an online chat room about what was happening to other people's cattle and learned our problem with the bull wasn't unusual. And he looked at how to collect the white stuff, the semen, from bulls.

His guess had been pretty good. There wasn't much choice other than to cut the bull's skin to expose what I guessed was its penis. Doc had asked him why he thought of doing the cutting. "It was pretty simple," Dad said and smiled. "In residency, I learned to do circumcisions—before we realized how much worse that makes things—and this was like circumcising a bull."

They laughed, but it was a forced laugh attempting to deny the seriousness of what was happening.

After the satellite lessons ended in late May, my typical day was to walk over to Cy and Martha's place after I'd done my chores. Since they'd become friends of my parents, their place was like an extension of ours. That is, until Millie arrived for the summer. I was excited to see her, but she immediately made it clear that I was a bore.

Still, the weather was good, and we all went to Valentine for the Fourth of July. The parade and the fireworks were as good as ever. In the car I tried in my clumsy way to make a conversation. Cy and Martha were polite and said things to help, but their words were as awkward as mine. Millie said next to nothing, and her silence made the air tense for the rest of us.

After that, the times I came over to Cy's in the afternoons, she didn't come out of her room much, and when she did her eyes were always a little pink like she had been crying. It was a thunderstorm that saved the last two weeks before she left.

Cy told me that when he was a boy, there would be pretty good rains, and occasionally thunderstorms.

Tornados happened sometimes, and it usually rained every couple of weeks except in the hottest part of the summer.

Now there were only one or two storms between May and September, and every storm was a thunderstorm. Whatever storm we had, it always brought high winds, huge amounts of rain, and tornados. The only thing that made living in north Nebraska possible was that most folks had relocated their buildings so that they, like us, were huddled next to some sort of hill that blunted the full force of the wind.

At the beginning of the summer, when they assumed that I would be playing a lot with Millie, Mom and Dad had made a plan to go to Valentine and leave me with Cy and Martha. Even though Millie obviously didn't want anything to do with me, Martha assured them it would still be okay for them to go. I think she was giving my parents a couple of days by themselves.

They were to be gone three nights. Some of it was for Dad to work on some new system with the other doctors in Valentine, but I'm pretty sure some if it was just for them to be in a different place when they didn't have time to take off to Omaha.

A storm was predicted to pass through South Dakota, maybe 200 miles north of us, but at the last minute some kind of warm front came up from the south just as the other front dipped down from the north. The result was a wild storm where the two fronts ran into each other right over us. Power went off in the first hour, but Martha had a lot of candles. The solar panels had kept the emergency batteries charged, and the satellite dish was unaffected in its recessed spot in the hillside, so we pretty much went on like a normal day except it was wet outside. We weren't expecting the tornado that started to pass to the east but then swung our way.

I heard the low roar, like a train, but I didn't know what it was. Cy did. He recognized the sound and yelled, "Oh, shit," as he jumped up. "Get to the cellar now!" He virtually threw Millie toward the door, and then stepped past her to open it. When she hesitated, he barked, "Millie! I said 'Now'!" I was almost as slow, and Martha looked around as though deciding what to grab, but by then we all heard the roar, and she took nothing.

My ears popped. I couldn't hear Cy for the noise, but the short high sound of glass shattering came out separate above the roar, and the house creaked. More glass shattered. The roar got real intense, and then, what seemed like an entire day later, the noise died down. But just when it seemed that the storm was going to leave us alone, water started coming down the steps into the cellar.

Cy decided that the danger from the tornado was over and climbed the stairs, but he couldn't open the door up into the house. So he came back down and went out the cellar door, up the steps, and then toward the barn.

It was still pouring, but the roar was gone. Despite the clouds, there was enough light left in the afternoon for him to see the barn, or what was left of it. One half was gone, and one half was there like it had been cut in half with a saw. Two cows were gone, and two were still in their stalls.

Cy got into the house through the front door and moved the pile of wet, broken chairs wedged against the door. The roof was okay, but half the windows were blown out and rain was pouring in. Martha and Millie went upstairs and got some clothes that were still dry. It was the same up there. Where there were windows, the rooms were dry like nothing had happened, but where the windows were gone, rain blew in and rolled down the stairs to the first floor and the basement below that.

By late afternoon, the rain quit and the sun came over the hill in their back yard. Their house was like ours because it was also supposed to be sheltered by the hill. "You can never prepare for everything," Cy said.

"Thank God we're all okay," Martha replied.

Dinner was huge. The refrigerator was off. Martha pointed to the food that was getting warm or thawing and said, "It'll all be rotten in a day or so. Might as well enjoy it while we can."

Martha found three sleeping bags in the attic. They were dry since the roof was okay and there was only one window up there, even though it had been blown out, too. She gave one to me and one to Millie. She and Cy shared the other one because their bed was mostly dry. Millie's bed was soaked, though, because it was by a broken window, so she and I slept in the living room.

"We'll see how bad it is when it dries out," Cy said about Millie's bed, "but that'll take a week or so. Sometimes they stink, and sometimes they dry out okay. You just have to wait and see."

The barnyard light was gone, so it was black dark after we turned out the flashlight. Millie and I lay on the floor. I could hear her breathing, but she'd still not said much. I felt I was only tolerated because Cy and Martha had volunteered to help my parents, and I figured I'd go on home and find something else to do as soon as Mom and Dad got back. But, as I was almost asleep, I heard Millie say in a defiant way, "I wish Mom's boyfriend got caught like the cow."

"Huh?" I asked. I wasn't sure I'd heard her correctly since she'd made no sense.

"I said, 'I wish Mom's boyfriend got caught like the cow.'"

"Oh. Okay."

"No. I mean it. I wish he was gone with the rain."

We lay there in the blackness. I could hear her breathe, but she sniffled a couple of times too. I sensed that she was crying, but I was afraid to say or do anything. She sniffed again, and this time it sounded very wet, like she was clearing out tears.

"I hate him. Every time Dad goes on a business trip, he shows up that night. He and Mom sit around in the kitchen, and after they think I'm asleep they go sit on the couch all night. Mom told me he's her friend from school, but not to tell Dad. I call him The Jerk. I always pray that he'll go away, but tonight I'm going to ask God if He can make it work like the cows. All at once would be even better."

For over a month I'd wanted Millie to talk to me, and now I couldn't think of any words to say back. I reached across and touched her shoulder. She sniffed one more time, and we both fell asleep from exhaustion.

"Let's go to the pool," Millie said at breakfast.

"What pool?" Martha asked.

I explained about the place where water collected in the creek bed and the old photo I'd found in the closet. "You're right," Cy added, "there used to be a pool there all the time—back when that city boy built your place—but the water was terribly cold. If they looked like they were relaxing, it must have been a really hot day! Those sure weren't hot springs."

"I brought a suit this year," Millie said to me.

I told her I didn't have a suit, but she said, "Wear your shorts. They're almost like a swimsuit."

—ɱ—

Millie had on a T-shirt and shorts over her swimsuit as we walked over the hill toward my parents' place. Water in the creek bed was running up onto the path more than I'd ever seen. I didn't think we'd get across okay, so we walked along Cy's side, going upstream to the pool. It was wider there, so the water didn't move as fast.

As I took off my shoes, Millie pulled her T-shirt over her head and slipped off her shorts. I was still too young to put a label on any sexual feelings as I watched her pull off her clothes. On that afternoon, however, taking off her clothes was an extension of revealing herself the night before, by her sharing her secret thoughts about her mom and The Jerk. We had only known each other last summer and a couple of weeks this summer, but the last barriers between us were almost gone. We were isolated from our peers, and we both needed a friend who was safe.

Now, when I think as a person who understands sex, I know what I could have also observed about how her body had changed over the year. Her tummy was still round like mine, but her hips were a little wider and her bottom a little rounder, and there were beginning bumps under the top of her plain blue swimsuit. But that summer, I only felt closer to her than to anyone but my parents.

We lay on the large rock to dry in the sun. I turned to

look at her, expecting to see that she was looking at the sky. But her eyes were closed, as though she had fallen asleep.

Impulsively, I raised myself on my elbow and kissed her lightly. That was how I expressed closeness to my parents and that was the only way I knew how.

She blinked and smiled. Then she said, "My mom kisses The Jerk like this." She put her lips on mine, held me with her hand on the back of my head and moved her face side to side. I instinctively closed my eyes, and then I heard the whir.

It wasn't a bird, or any insect I'd heard before, and it took a moment to locate the sound coming from above us. There it was, a drone, like a small four-rotor helicopter, circling above us.

Millie grabbed her shirt. "What the fuck do you want?" she yelled at it, shocking me with her language. She picked up a rock and threw it, but the drone was too high for that. I threw a rock myself.

The drone circled lazily to prove we were impotent, and then it flew on up the stream toward where the water had come from. When we told Cy about it at dinner, he said, "I'd heard the water people were doing a survey with drones. I hope they don't see your dad's dam."

But they did.

Our community was too small even to call it a hamlet. We were fifty miles from the nearest major highway, and the only clue that other people had lived there was an old house in which the first floor had been converted to a small store. A single gas pump for regular gas had been installed at the side, not even out front. They sold so little gas that the trailer truck came only three times a year to refill the above-ground tanks.

This house was also where the rural delivery dropped off mail. There was no letter carrier to deliver mail to individual farms and homes. Lucy, the woman who tended the store, never sorted the mail. You just came in and she looked through the pile to see if there was a letter or magazine for you. With everyone on the Internet, there wasn't much more than magazines.

About a month after Millie went back to Omaha, Mom went to Lucy's and brought Dad a letter from the Sioux Falls Water District.

"Shit. They saw the dam," he said as he laid the unopened letter on the table.

"What'll you do?" asked Mom.

"Nothing." He pointed to the table. "If I haven't read their letter, I don't have to respond to it. Let's see what they do first."

We didn't need to wait long.

On Monday, a deputy sheriff and a man who wasn't wearing a uniform showed up just after breakfast. Everyone liked my dad, and you could tell the deputy didn't want to be there.

I listened as Dad talked to them outside. The man said he represented the Sioux Falls Water Department. "The water belongs to us, Mr. Kobb," he said. "You're stealing our water with your dam."

"Fuck that," Dad said. He was cussing again. "It's rain that fell on my land, so it's my water."

"Not really. You own the land, but we own the rights to all the water. The only water you own is what seeps into the ground. The water that becomes part of the ground is yours, and you get that out with a well."

"Two problems with that, Mr. Whatever-your-name-is. One, what we can get from the well is hardly enough to live on. And, two, the well's getting foul. It's those chemicals from fracking everywhere. You probably let the frackers poison the water."

"Those are not our problems, Mr. Kobb," the man said. As he spoke, he somehow made our family name sound like he was belittling my dad.

"Why's this the first I've heard of this?"

"I can't explain why you're ignorant ..." he let the insult hang in the air. "Water rights were put in place before any individual owned this land other than the government. Our rights come before yours, and they come directly from the government."

Dad slowly squeezed his hands into fists, and then just as slowly extended his fingers and patted them on the sides of his legs. "Well, I think for now I'll just leave it, and you can try to do something about it."

The sheriff's deputy had not said anything up to that point, but he stepped to my dad's side, put a hand on his shoulder and coaxed him to turn around so their backs were to the man from Sioux Falls but they were closer to me. "Doc," he began respectfully. "I can only guess how you feel, but they mean business and if you try to fight them, you will lose. It won't be me who comes here with them. It'll be federal guys."

In the end, the only defiance left to my dad was to refuse to bulldoze the dam himself. "If you don't like it, you can take it out," and he went inside the house and slammed the door. And that's what the Sioux Falls Water Department did a week later.

They called to tell us that their team with a bulldozer would be there right after lunch. Dad gritted his teeth and did not reply. He handed the phone to me, "Tell them we heard them." He left our farm before 11:00, and did not return until long after they were gone.

In September, Dad got his annual supply of flu vaccine. "You want to help me?" he asked.

"Sure."

He showed me how to put on gloves, wipe the bottle top with alcohol, and fill a syringe with half a milliliter of vaccine. Wipe again, and repeat.

Everyone had to come to Lucy's for mail, so Dad always gave flu shots in the back of the store. On the way there, he explained the importance of a new syringe for everyone so that we didn't carry germs called bacteria from one person's arm to someone else. He also explained how the alcohol wipe on the skin kept the needle from pulling germs from the skin inside to make an infection.

Everyone accepted my being there and helping. Other kids were learning how to manage cattle and run chickens like their parents, so it was logical for me to start being an apprentice to my dad. And I didn't do any part that would be dangerous if I got it wrong.

Ronnie and Charles were both among those who came in. As they rolled up their sleeves, I had a thought that I'd like to bend the tip to blunt the needle Dad used for Charlie, but I knew Dad would be extremely upset if he thought that I'd done that. He had pride in his work. He might even have made me apologize to Charlie myself.

Instead, I nodded when he held his arm out and took comfort in the fact that for once he wouldn't dare try to hurt me or humiliate me, not in front of my dad.

Dad and I didn't go with the other dads and sons to camp the night before deer season opened. I hadn't told him about Charles grabbing me, but he could tell that there was some very deep reason that I didn't want to do that again. He arranged to need to go to Valentine that weekend. Ronnie's dad offered to take me with them, but Dad made up some additional excuse to let me go with him.

It was just as well that I wasn't there. There were no deer to be seen, and one of the dads got drunk and there was a brawl when the other dads tried to get him to shut up. Some of the dads took their sons and left in the middle of the night, and most of the others left before breakfast in the morning.

That was the year that only one person shot a deer. No one knew why, but there were no deer to find anywhere.

Encrypted portable document format—ePDF for short—made it possible to validate electronic documents as good as a notary. So ePDFs made pretty much all paper documents obsolete. But Dad had another approach. He liked paper. He collected paper.

Over time, he filled one of the unused bedrooms, the biggest one, with books and paper printed copies of medical stuff and books he said he just liked to have around.

He took me in there sometimes and would pull out a book or a paper and hold it. "I like the feel of paper," he said. "Paper's been around for several thousand years, the computer screen less than two hundred. I'm still waiting to see which one wins out."

This was the room where he'd had his microscope, but now he kept that down in the living room. It was more convenient to bring it to the kitchen to follow the progress of his experiments.

After struggling with the bull semen, his goal was to not get in that situation again, and he'd decided to run his own experiments to see if he could find a good way to keep sperm wiggling. He tried all sorts of mixtures such as honey by itself and honey mixed with water. He made his own sugar water, and he tried it with and without a dash of salt. He also tried the egg yolk, the egg white, and both together.

He made the mixtures in the evening, just before bedtime, and we'd look in the morning to see if the semen still wiggled. By this time, he'd taught me that the wiggling was little things called sperm in the whitish semen. More often than not, the wiggling had stopped by morning. After he'd run a new experiment, he'd let me look first. "Well, what do you see?"

"I'm not certain." I'd try to avoid committing myself because I knew how important the answer was to him, and I didn't want to be wrong.

"Not an option. You've got to decide what you think. That's how you learn to stand by what you believe. Right or wrong, and if you're wrong, it's good practice in how to change your mind gracefully."

Finally he came back to using a scrambled egg like the one he'd intuitively called for the first time. "It makes sense," he said. "The egg is growing a new chicken and the sperm are growing new cattle. It must be a mixture Mother Nature made for new life."

He got excited one day when he realized he'd kept sperm alive in our refrigerator for almost a week and they started moving when he brought the mixture to room temperature in a pan of warm water. He pulled me to his microscope, "Look, you can see them. Like the critters from the creek bed."

I looked and agreed. After that he experimented with keeping sperm moving longer and longer times. I never asked where the sperm came from since we didn't have a bull, but it's pretty obvious when I think about it now.

Dad had said I could look at any of his books in the upstairs bedroom that I wanted. One book had a lot of line drawings of how people are put together. They showed the skeleton and muscles, and the guts and stuff. The thing that made this book different from all his other ones was that the drawings showed people standing or lying like they would normally, but the skin had been taken off to show the muscles, or the stomach was opened up to show the guts. He said it was a collection of classic anatomic drawings made hundreds of years ago, and that was the way they used to make drawings to record what they'd seen. The man who cut open the body drew what he saw in a dead person, but to make it acceptable to others, he drew it as though the person was casually standing there.

One of the pictures was by a guy named Leonardo something or other. It was drawn as though a man and a woman were cut in half as they were hugging each other. At the bottom of the picture, the penis of the man went into the woman. At least I interpreted it that way because that's what happened when the penis of the bull came out. Dad wasn't there to ask the day I found that picture.

We had another storm in March. Dad explained that the days were getting longer, so there was more sun to warm the air, and that the difference in the heat in the air made the storm. Cy and Martha had fixed their broken windows from the big storm, and this one wasn't supposed to be as big. The wind blew in bursts against my window. There was some lightning, but not as much as with the storm with the tornado. I fell asleep listening to the rain. We'd be okay inside our house.

In the middle of the night, Dad woke me up. "Jack, get dressed." He was very serious.

I mumbled, "Huh?"

"I need you to help me. Cy called and Martha is very sick."

Mom was downstairs in her robe as we put on raincoats in the kitchen. "You be careful," she said to Dad.

"Don't worry."

We took Dad's pickup and drove the long way going on the road to Cy and Martha's because Dad didn't want to try to cross the creek at night after rain. The wiper exposed the road in short flashes, but we both knew the way well, and it was pretty unlikely anyone else would be out that time of night in a rain like that.

Between focusing on sharp turns and watching for flooding, Dad explained, "From what Cy said, Martha's real sick. He's going to need you to help him."

"Why?"

"I think Martha needs to get to Omaha. He needs to go with her, and someone needs to do the chores in the morning." By this time we'd turned down Cy's road, and I could see the lights in his yard.

"Stay close and do what I tell you," were the last words Dad said as he grabbed his bag and rushed into the house. He was inside by the time I'd closed the door behind me.

Martha was in her bed and pale, as pale as Mom had been when she got sick. Dad pulled out a hand drill like the one the paramedic had used on Mom. I guess he'd learned to do it himself. He had bags that looked like water in his case.

"She just woke me up and said she had this horrible pain in her stomach," said Cy, "and right away it burned to her back, and she got real pale."

"You called the air ambulance folks?" Dad asked to confirm his direction to Cy had been followed.

"The moment we hung up."

The bag of liquid was going into Martha's shoulder. "Shit night to find us," Dad commented. Martha gazed around the room but I don't think she recognized Dad or me. Cy sat by her and rubbed her hand lightly. We waited. As the local doctor, Dad was provided a homing radio so they could send the paramedics to wherever he was, and pretty soon we could hear the whap, whap, whap of the helicopter.

"I'm pretty sure she's got a leaking aneurysm," Dad told one of the paramedics as they were loading her on the stretcher. "They can't do much in Valentine. Do you have enough fuel for Omaha?"

"I'll confirm with Joel, but I'm pretty sure we do," the paramedic replied, and as they finished getting her into the patient bay, he yelled over the noise of the engine, "Yep. We can do Omaha."

"Then let's go," Dad said. He and Cy both started to get on, but the pilot stopped them, "We can do Omaha, but we'll need to limit our weight. One extra, not two."

Cy paused and looked at Martha. Then he kissed her cheek and said to Dad, "You go with her. You can do something. I can't. I'll be right along behind you." Dad closed the door, and Cy crossed himself as he watched the helicopter rise into the rain and yelled after them even though they couldn't hear him, "You take good care of her."

I didn't notice how wet and cold we were until the lights couldn't be seen anymore. "Okay," Cy turned to me. "Let me show you what to do." Cy showed me where to feed his cows and how to take care of the chickens. It was a quick lesson in all that needed to be done twice a day at his place, and I was going to be doing that for however long he was with Martha. Dad had figured that from what Cy said on his initial phone call.

Our place was on Cy's way to Omaha. He drove me up our driveway and stopped only long enough for me to jump out. Mom was waiting with hot tea for both of us, but Cy was gone too quickly for us to share it with him. He had a four-hour drive in good weather, but it was raining hard again.

The next morning, the rained tapered off, and Mom drove me over to do the chores Cy had shown me. I didn't know it yet, but I would be doing them for a couple of months. Two days later, Dad took the bus from Omaha to Mitchell, and Mom and I drove up to pick him up.

Martha survived her surgery, but she'd been in shock so long that no one was certain what would happen to her. She seemed to get better about a week later, but then she got bad over the next couple of weeks and died.

The day of her funeral, Mom, Dad, and I were up at 3:00 in the morning to tend to the animals before we left. The weather wasn't bad, but we barely made it to the services at 11:00. Cy was pretty broken up. Millie was with him. Millie's mom and dad were together, but they didn't hug each other like a lot of the rest of the folks.

I saw Millie, but only for a few minutes. There wasn't anyone covering Dad's patients, and we had to be back to take care of the evening chores on both farms. Despite our intentions, we lingered longer than Dad had expected and didn't get back until after dark.

Cy stayed in Omaha after Martha's funeral. Dad said he was sorting things out. I kept on doing the chores. Cy's barn was still in bad shape.

That was when I met Horace, a handyman or as Dad said, "Jack-of-all-trades," who was rebuilding the part of Cy's barn that had been blown away by the tornado. Horace worked for a lot of folks, but he hadn't worked for my parents yet. That would come.

It didn't make sense to keep cows at Cy's if he wasn't there all the time, so Dad eventually used his truck to bring them over to our barn. We left the chickens on their own. When the days became warmer, Mom stopped driving me over, and I walked over every afternoon to check on them.

Dad was not a ball player. I didn't think he'd played organized ball sports in his life. Mom, on the other hand, loved sports. One time we raced and she jumped over a log like it was the most natural thing. I asked how she'd done that, and she told me she'd run over hurdles on a team when she was in college.

And Mom was determined that I would play on sports teams. So when some of the dads organized a softball practice after the last snow melted and the ground dried, she insisted that I be part of the group and drove me to the field on Saturday afternoon.

Because Dad had never thought to play catch with me, I had no experience in how to position my hands to catch a ball that was coming toward my face, instead of being hit in the face.

The dads lined boys up in two rows facing each other.

We threw balls to a partner in line right across from us. At first my partner didn't throw too fast. I managed to catch a slow throw, or at other times to look like I'd just missed it or mistimed my response. But I was barely keeping up while everyone else was warming up. Then the dads stepped up the pace.

I had a glove on my left hand, but I was clumsy and the second time I tried to catch a faster pitch, I miscalculated and the ball hit the bare fingertips of my right hand. It pulled the flesh back from the underside of the nail on two fingers. They hurt and they bled. Impulsively, I shook my hand, and I couldn't stop a few tears.

"What's wrong, Kobb?" a dad asked.

I held up my fingers to show him, expecting at least some minor sympathy, but he took a look and said, "That's what happens when you don't keep your eye on the ball." He looked closer. "You bite your fingernails, don't you? Now you'll stop."

I was humiliated because I did bite my nails when I was nervous and I'd been nervous for the days leading up to that Saturday. I also didn't know then that it's physiologically impossible to turn your eyes fast enough to follow a ball. It can't be done for anything more than a slow toss. The rest of the time, following the ball relies on making a good guess on where the ball will be a few milliseconds later.

You learn how to make an excellent guess by throwing and catching a ball enough times to learn how a ball will travel and what it will do after it leaves the hand of the thrower, pitcher or fielder, or another player. It makes no sense to say to keep your eye on the ball.

There was no option but to keep trying, but I didn't get better and only felt more pain in my fingertips. Charles noticed and threw faster at me. It was a miserable afternoon.

Dad wasn't much help. He was late picking me up so one of the dads had to wait with me until Dad got there. The bleeding under my nails had stopped by the time he arrived, and when he asked how it was, all I could say was that it wasn't very much fun. I'd have loved to ask him to practice tossing a ball around with me, but I knew already that it would be harder for him than for me.

I was ecstatic when it rained the next Friday and the field was too wet to play on Saturday.

A couple weeks later, Cy drove his truck up from Omaha and stayed overnight on his place. The next day he came over and met two men who'd arranged to buy his cows that Dad had kept in our barn. Dad hadn't tried to service any of the cows to get pregnant that spring because of the stress of Cy's absence and us already taking care of his animals. And cows drink a lot of water, so loss of the dam made watering more animals hard.

Cy also sold the men his tractor, but no one wanted to buy the chickens, so he gave them to me. He said he wouldn't be back in the summer, so Millie wasn't coming either. I was sad, sadder than I'd ever have expected, although it was logical to miss a friend.

Just before school started, I had to go to Omaha to get my glasses adjusted. Mom drove me down so Dad wouldn't need to worry about who was covering for him. She also sent Millie's mom a text that we were coming and asked if we could all go for ice cream. We had Millie's address and after my appointment drove to an area that had a lot of uncut, dry grass in some yards, and a car parked in a yard down the street. Cy met us at the door, and I was happy to see him.

The day was very hot and the humidity felt like 100%, so Mom appreciated it that Cy's new place was air-conditioned. She'd only met Millie's mom at the funeral because, although Millie's mom had grown up on Cy's place, she had married and moved away before we moved up from Omaha.

The closest place to get ice cream was a small cafe two blocks from Millie's house. Her mom assured my mom that we could walk there without an adult. There was no one else on the street. The trees were big enough to cast a shadow on half the sidewalk, but it didn't protect us from the heat. I was sweating, and my shirt was wet on my back. As we walked along, Millie started to talk, "It's better with granddad here."

"How's it better?"

"Dad's still on the road about every week," Millie explained, "but The Jerk doesn't show up as soon as Dad's out of the house any more. I think he knows granddad wouldn't like it." She laughed. "Probably knows he'd kill him ..." Abruptly she lightened her comments. "... and granddad reads to me a lot. He makes different voices and stories get to be fun when he tells them."

Millie talked in a deep voice and held her hands over her head like claws as she imitated how Cy sounded. I laughed. There were no cows or chickens, but for a few minutes I imagined we were at home walking to our house from Cy's farm. Millie went on to talk about her new school and the real swimming pools in Omaha.

I wanted to say something about how great it was to see her, but we got to the shop and talked about what kind of ice cream we liked instead.

That fall no one talked much about deer season. At class on Thursday afternoon, some of the guys talked about how their dads got out their guns and cleaned them. One guy's dad had given him a new hunting rifle. "It's got an electronic telescope sight, like snipers use in the army," he bragged.

"We better paint all the cows orange," another guy teased him. "A big fancy gun like that you're likely to think anything is a deer, even if it moos." I laughed with everyone else, but I hoped they wouldn't come on our place to hunt. Dad told me one time that a high power rifle bullet could travel over two miles.

The thing missing from the conversation was that no one talked about scouting out where they planned to go the first day. By the end of a typical September, the serious hunters had walked miles of woods and near streams looking for deer tracks. If they were lucky, they'd seen a buck that they would try to shoot once season opened. They always lied about where they had been scouting so no one else would go get their deer before they did.

None of that happened that year. Opening day came and went with little fanfare, and no one was bringing in skins and meat to brag about. Finally one man shot a three-point buck, but he was so horrified when he started to dress the animal, he dragged it to the back of his truck and brought it to Doc Porter. When Doc Porter had looked at the animal, he called Dad. I went along.

We pulled up in Doc Porter's yard and walked over to the group that was standing around the dead animal.

The hunter had shot the deer and then pulled it up on a tree to field dress it. The rope he'd used to lift the legs was still on the animal's hind feet. The butt hole had been cut free, and there was a cut up the middle of the stomach that he'd made before he quit.

"He ain't got no dick, Doc," said the hunter, unaware of how funny that could sound to anyone just listening to him. "He's got balls, but no dick."

Doc Porter knelt down and squeezed the buck where his penis should have been. Dad kneeled beside him and felt, too. Neither one of them said a thing when they stopped because they both knew what they had to do next.

"Do you want to do this, doc?" Doc Porter asked my dad.

"No, this is more your field than mine," Dad answered. "I'm here as an extra set of hands."

Doc Porter nodded and picked up a knife to cut crossways where the hunter had started to cut open the abdomen. He poked around with the tip of his knife to find the hole where the penis should have come out. Then he cut along the bottom of the deer back from the hole he'd made to open the whole area up. Way at the bottom he found a little nub of pink flesh. He poked this around and said, "Looks like this is all there is."

"Damn," said Dad. "It's gotten into the deer, too."

I looked at Dad. He looked at me but shook his head

slightly and made like his lips were whispering silently to me, "Later. Talk later." He turned to Doc Porter. Both docs stood up and thought for a few minutes about what to do next. Finally, Doc Porter said, "We better call the game warden. Tell him to cancel hunting season 'til we get this sorted out."

No one said anything. We all listened as Doc Porter spoke to the game warden. "Yep. Yes. No, it's just like the boys. Well, it's your choice, but I think we need to stop everything until we know what's happening." He listened to the game warden talk for a long time before he replied, "Yeah. I'll take the heat. Blame me if you need to cover your ass."

He ended the call but none of us knew what to say, so we said nothing. We knew we had seen something very important—important, but not good. It was like folks said they felt when the dike broke and New York flooded the final time.

I knew that I'd remember what I'd seen.

Just before Christmas, we had sex education as part of science classes. Boys and girls met with Mr. Martin in separate groups. Because of the way grades were grouped in sets of three, each guy had the same lesson three years in a row. This was my first time, but it was the third time for the oldest guys in this class.

Mr. Martin turned on a projector to show an animated

drawing like a cartoon of a little girl. As she got taller, she grew breasts and got hair about the same place that I had a few hairs by my penis. Then the camera moved in close to focus on drawings of the uterus and ovaries. The voice of the movie explained how the ovaries released an egg and then made a hormone—it started with a "P" I think—that made the uterus ready to grow a baby. If a sperm swam up and met the egg, together they'd make a baby, but if there was no baby, the egg gave up doing its job to make the uterus ready. Then the insides of the uterus fell out, and there was bleeding when that happened. That was called a something-or-another period. I caught the word period, but not the first word.

Sperm were made in the testicles of a boy, but the drawings only showed the testicles and nothing else, and there was no explanation for how the sperm got close to an egg. One of Ronnie's friends raised his hand, "How does the sperm get to the egg? Float around through the air?" Mr. Martin was flustered by the question and mumbled something vague about "special ways" that sperm get from a husband to his wife when they decide to have a baby.

Out in the schoolyard, one of the guys two grades ahead of me decided to show off what he knew. "It's simple. When it's time to have a baby, they make the man's testicle cold so it stops feeling and cut out a little piece of a testicle with a sperm in it. Then they put it with an egg and that grows inside a woman."

The other guys paid close attention as he continued. "They used to do it the old way, but a guy had to worry about getting a girl pregnant and, if she did, he had to stop dating other girls."

One of the older guys challenged him. "What do you mean 'the old way'?"

"Well, they got together in a bed or something and the sperm only had a little distance to go," the first guy said defensively. "My cousin, he's older, he told me how that worked." But he kept fumbling for an explanation and talking louder in an effort to intimidate the other guys into not asking more questions because he hadn't asked his cousin to explain any further and didn't know much more than we did. He just knew how to pretend he knew something everyone else didn't.

I remembered Dad's drawing by the Leonardo guy showing a way for a boy and girl to be connected closer than just lying beside each other. It was clear to me that the sperm that were animated coming to the egg in the movie looked and behaved a lot like the sperm in the semen that Dad showed me under his microscope. And I worried even more about my defective penis that I couldn't talk to anyone about, even my dad.

I understood better what had gone on with the bull, and why dad and Doc Porter had worried when the buck didn't have a real penis. At least it made some sense to me when Dad said that he and Doc Porter were going to try to catch a buck and a doe to breed a deer like they did cattle. Good idea, but much more difficult to accomplish than they expected.

The idea was to get men, hunters during the off-season, to capture deer alive, but that failed pretty quickly. They could track a deer and corner it, but the first time they succeeded in putting a rope on a deer, it went wild bucking and tearing around until it caught one of the ropes as it tried to escape jumping over a fallen tree and broke its neck. The hunters had been so excited that they were going to save their deer season, and next thing you know, they were speechless.

The drone from the Sioux Falls water department flew over our place a couple times a year to check that Dad didn't rebuild his dam. They didn't, however, anticipate that Dad figured if there was a way around their stupid water rights, he would find it. Whatever he did had to look like he was using our well.

He gave up on getting enough water for more cattle, and focused on better water for us to use in the house. This meant that the biggest problem was how to get water from the creek to our house and not be obvious about it. The solution came from a pipe he found sticking up from the ground in an abandoned field near the creek bed. The rancher who'd built the house had built an irrigation system but never used the pipes because the water level dropped soon after they moved in. The pipes had been there long enough that they were no longer visible from the air, and they went all the way from the pump house by our house to the field—or the other way around if you wanted to run water from the field to our house.

The next challenge was to get water from the creek bed without building a dam. Dad spent hours looking at the rocks by the dry pool where I'd been with Millie after the rain. That area had a lot of water for a day or two after it rained, and the water level got almost up to the top of the rocks on either side of the creek, high enough to cover the area under the rocks for a day or so. That was where he could get water without a dam.

Dad figured he would need a holding tank so he talked to neighbors about how he was going to improve the septic leach field on our property. Everyone would expect him to be doing construction. When he ordered materials, he ordered two extra septic tanks and had Horace and Jonathan work together to bury them next to the house like the two tanks that we were going to use for toilet water and stuff. The tanks were big enough that I could stand up in one. Horace didn't like the idea of someone claiming they owned Dad's water any more than Dad did, and they worked as a team of rebels.

Jonathan ran the backhoe, Horace called directions to guide the tanks into place, and Dad supervised.

To get the water from the creek bed, they dug a small trench by hand and buried a pipe around the rock by the pool so that it was open underneath the rock but couldn't be seen by the drone. The bushes were big enough to conceal their pipe almost all the way up to the field where they connected it to the old irrigation pipe. Only about twenty feet of open field was disturbed by the new pipe, and Dad and Horace laid that section of pipe in a winding way so it wouldn't look so manmade. After that they could only hope that the drone operators wouldn't notice that small stretch of new digging.

The last challenge was to get the water up from the pool after a rain and into the pipe to go downhill to the extra tank. They needed a pump by the creek, but a pump would need a wire. Their solution was to install the pump and a small gas generator hidden under a tree that was started by hand when the pool was full. Eventually, that became my job.

The water we got that way was still muddy from the rain, but no one grew crops around there anymore so it was free of chemicals. Dad's plan was that the muddy water went to the first tank, where the dirt settled out over a week or so. Then a small pump transferred the clear water to the second tank that we drank from. It wasn't enough water to waste any, but it was enough that we drank clean water if we used the separate faucet Horace put in beside the sink in the kitchen. Dad used power from new solar panels to run the small pumps between the tanks by our house.

The first time we turned the water on, we clinked our glasses and sat around like we were sampling a special wine.

Two cows had calves in early spring. Doc Porter gave the usual vaccinations, but Dad still wondered if there was a better way to get them pregnant. The vet school farm near Omaha had been working on a method that was used to help couples to have babies years ago where they would anesthetize the balls—Dad wanted me to call them testicles—and take a little tiny bit of the testicle and try to get just a couple of sperm out and then put them with an egg from the cow's ovary. It worked, but the person doing it had to do all that work under a microscope. It was complicated to get the egg from a woman's ovary when she wanted to get pregnant, and even more complicated to get one from a cow.

After he'd tried to work out a plan in his head, Dad decided that it would be harder to get an egg from a cow than to get the sperm from a male testicle. "A woman who goes through getting an egg out of her, well she usually wants to have a kid and you can talk to her. A cow you can't talk to in any way she'll know what you're up to. We just don't have the money to get it done at the vet school," he concluded. "But we've gotten two calves this year."

That was so like Dad, or like anyone who lived in the land that God forgot to water: Everything is improvising and trying to get something to work out.

Shortly after the calves were born, Kobb showed up again. This time he arrived in the late afternoon and walked into the kitchen like he lived there and had only been gone overnight. The next morning, he made pancakes for everyone and cleaned up the kitchen, including a pan Mom had left after dinner. "You don't need to do that," she said.

"It's my part of the room and board," he replied. "Want to be sure to keep my welcome." Then he said to me, as though telling me something I would never have known, "You never want to wear out your welcome. It's like parts for that old bike of mine, they're real hard to replace if they wear out."

He stood and patted my shoulder. "Speaking of replacement parts," he pointed out to his motorcycle, "you want to help me work on my bike?"

"Chores," Mom reminded me. "Then help granddad."

By the time I'd finished my chores, Kobb had spread a tarp on the ground for a workspace. He'd removed the seat and exhaust pipe and emptied the gas tank, and he was wiping dirt and grease off the engine. "This machine will do great about anywhere you want to take her," he said, "but you need to be careful not to get dirt inside her. First thing before I open anything up is to clean her skin as shiny as the day she came off the line."

He repeated himself as he worked because it was slow going to clean the whole engine before he started removing parts, and since there was nothing else to talk about, it filled the time. "She'll do great off road or on the highway, doesn't matter how much dirt's on the outside. It's the inside where she can get hurt."

Kobb seemed to be talking about two things. The motorcycle in front of him was obvious, but when he talked about hurting her inside, it was like that time he talked about Jack. He got a glassy-eyed look that left me wondering for just a second what else he was thinking about.

"You ever seen the inside of one of these?" he asked.

"No."

"Well, there's lots of parts, but in the end they're real simple."

He named the things as he removed them. "This is the spark plug." He held up a round thing, about the size of his little finger, white in the middle and black at both ends. "Ignition wire," a black wire about a foot long. "Cylinder head bolts." He worked a wrench back and forth and removed each bolt, one at a time.

Kobb worked with machines like Dad worked with animals, and I thought about the microscope and looking at the little living things. "Dad has a microscope," I said. "He told me it belonged to you."

Kobb didn't look up or pause in his motions. "Yep. That was a long time ago." He lifted up a large piece of metal, removing it from the top of the engine, and a round, can-like thing wobbled in the air on top of a metal piece. "That's the piston." He pointed to the blackened top of the piston, "It's got some serious wear, but no way to fix that now."

He put his finger into a hole on the side of the piston, felt around on both sides, and then, working a wrench back and forth, took out a smaller round cylinder with its own hole in the middle, sort of a tube or a short piece of pipe. "That's the wrist pin," he continued as the pin came out and he lifted the piston off where it had been attached, "and its bearing."

He named the piston rod that stuck up from below and tucked a pink rag around the rod. "That keeps anything from falling into the crankshaft underneath. Drop something in there and you need to take the whole thing apart. You only forget once on that."

"Dad said you used the microscope in medical school."

"Yes, I did."

"Are you a doctor?"

"I was."

"What kind of doctor are you?"

"I was a gynecologist."

"What's a gynecologist do?"

"Helps a woman have babies, and takes care of cancers that can get in there."

I'd heard the word cancer, but I'd never known anyone who had cancer. The only sick people I'd seen were Mom and Martha. "What's cancer? I've heard the word, but what is it?"

Kobb had the piston on the ground and was taking off a little metal band that was wrapped around it. He didn't stop or look up from what he was doing, but he slowed down a lot. "Cancer is like getting dirt in this bike. Everything can look fine, but it's all wrong on the inside."

He held up the band he'd taken off the piston. "Piston ring. Such a little thing, but when it goes bad, she loses all her strength." He didn't say anything more. I guess I was too dumb to keep quiet, so I asked, "Why aren't you a doctor anymore?"

"I couldn't do it after she died. Your grandmother. After your grandmother died." He looked as if he was thinking about the past as much as he was answering me. I'd fallen into questions that I wished I had left alone, and made up my mind to stop asking anything and to ask Mom later, but Kobb kept talking on his own. "I gave her the pill. It was the newest and best." He was talking to me, but he looked away as if I'd see what he saw if I looked the same direction.

Everyone in the family except me knew the story. I think he'd figured I had to find out sometime and decided he would tell me himself. "After your dad was born, we planned to wait a couple of years to have our next child. They've taught you about babies in school, haven't they?"

"Yes. This year."

"So you know about ovaries." He built on what he assumed I'd learned. "There are pills that stop the ovary from making an egg until you're ready."

"Uh, huh," I said to show that I was paying attention.

"There was this new pill, a great new pill. But it had an effect on other parts of her body. She looked fine, but we couldn't get pregnant again after she stopped the pill, and then one day, years later, she was terribly ill. Drugs, radiation, hair falling out, none of it worked. Six months start to finish. And I'd given her the pills." He stared out the open door of the barn. "Actually, I'd asked the drug rep for some free samples."

Kobb was the man I remembered when I was very small, so this meant the woman with no hair was my grandmother. Six months! She was tender with me even though she was dying. I remembered losing her comfort, and I had never even known her like Kobb had. I couldn't decide if I'd intruded where I wasn't welcome or if Kobb appreciated that someone listened to him talk about her, even if the person listening was only eleven years old and didn't understand a lot of adult things.

It took Kobb a little over a week to put back together everything he'd taken apart. Then he put the gas back in the tank, replaced the engine oil, and put his weight down hard on the pedal to kick-start the engine. The bike started on the second try. "You gotta' drive it easy for the first few hundred miles," he said. "It's like breaking in a brand new engine."

The rest of the day, there wasn't much to do before evening chores and supper. We walked to where the pool would collect after rain. The creek was dry because it hadn't rained for awhile, but Kobb said how clever Dad was to hide the pipe under the rock and the generator under a bush. "I'll come back to see it in action when you've had a good rain."

After dinner I went out with him to close the barn up for the night. He checked his bike before we locked the door. "Not likely anyone'll be here trying to steal it tonight, but who knows, those new piston rings are pretty valuable."

I laughed and he pushed my shoulder in an affectionate way. "What was grandmother's name?" I asked impulsively.

"Sarah."

"What'd she look like?"

"Tall … strong … a lot like your mother, only she had blonde hair. Beautiful long blonde hair." His mood got sad for a moment, but then he snapped out of it. "Look how you've got me talking! She was beautiful. Funny. Could make me laugh on the worst day. Everyone loved her. And I knew I was safe with her."

We said good night, and we left our doors to the bathroom ajar. I woke up to the noise of him starting his motorcycle in the early hours of the morning, long before sunrise.

That fall, I was officially in the seventh grade. Mom had not given up her idea that I'd play on a sports team. When some of the dads organized a basketball team that practiced after school the days we all were at the schoolhouse, she encouraged me to join. I was over six feet tall, and still growing, so everyone assumed I'd be a great basketball player. I might have if I'd understood, or actually really believed, that I could get better if I practiced.

I can't say it was Dad's fault that I didn't practice

around our house, but that would have been more likely to happen if there'd been a basketball hoop. But there wasn't one until late fall, just before we started playing other schools, when Mom insisted Dad put a basket on a board in front of the barn. Obviously, there wasn't a floor to dribble on, but Mom had me practice shooting baskets from all over the place, even without bouncing the ball before I shot. To encourage me, she stood near the goal and threw each ball back for me to try again.

I learned to shoot a fair free throw, but most of the rest of the time I wasn't very good. I was, however, the tallest guy on our team, so I was useful on defense under the goal, until I fouled out. That happened because it was hard for me to get a good feel for how to hold my hand in front of a guy and not touch the guy himself. Players or coaches on other teams quickly saw this weakness, and when I put up my hand, opponents intentionally drove in to draw a foul.

When Dad finally came to a game, and I fouled out in the third quarter, he saw what Mom had been trying to explain. On the drive home, he explained the problem to me different from how our coach had tried to explain it. To Dad, the goal was to stop thinking about how to avoid the foul, and instead to think like I was flashing my hand in front of the other guy, long enough to throw his shot off but not long enough to make contact. "You remember that game we played when you were young?"

he asked. "You held your ears, and I held my hands out in front, and you'd try to bring your hands down fast enough to hit my hands?"

"Uh, huh. "

"It's like that. Get your hands in and out in front of the other guy, but don't let him touch you."

I was puzzled about how that was similar to our game.

"He's trying to get so close that you touch him," he explained, "But what he's really trying to do is run into you. He doesn't care if you hit him or he runs into you. If your hand touches his body, it's a foul on you the same as if you'd hit him. So it's like the game with your hands. Get in front of him, but get out before he can run into you."

Dad's explanation helped me not foul out every time I played center, and he taught me something else. "You can't stop it every time a guy runs toward the basket. But you shouldn't try either. If you try every time, you'll keep touching him and you'll foul out. Your job is to be part of a team and to slow the other guy down.

"What wins the game is the team. It's like if you want green, you mix blue and yellow. You can't just keep adding more blue or more yellow by itself. Mixtures do what individuals can't."

Dad was making one of his comparisons again. He called them metaphors.

Our team still didn't score a lot, but at least I stopped

fouling out, and the dad who was the coach said that was helpful. Just before Christmas, we won our first game. Mom was jumping around and kissed Dad in her excitement. I wasn't a sports hero, but at least I wasn't the team's biggest problem anymore.

For Christmas, Mom and Dad gave me a kit to make a telescope. It had a six-inch mirror, the long tube, and a tripod to hold it up.

Dad had let me use his field glasses to look at the sky, and you could see how many more stars there were than I could see with my eyes alone. "But you need to have a way to collect the light to see the smaller stars," he explained. "The front of the field glasses are about two inches across, so you can focus all the light that hits a two inch circle."

"But with the mirror, you can use all the light that hits this six inch piece of glass. Remember your geometry, with the two inch lens, you get the light from ..." He paused to think to himself. "... let's see, two inch diameter ... so, one inch radius ... one squared is one, then one times pi ... you get the light that comes in just over three square inches."

I struggled to follow as he continued, "With the six inch mirror ... three inch radius ... three squared is nine ... multiply by pi ... about 27 square inches ... You get nine times more light to see with."

"Oh."

I hadn't followed his geometry exactly, but when the telescope was assembled, it was like someone had turned on a light to let us see more stars and see them brighter. The Milky Way was like a light show.

"Let's look at Orion's belt," he suggested. "It's really great, but it won't be up for awhile." So he set an alarm and at three in the morning he woke me up and, once we'd bundled up for the cold, we went outside.

"Orion's a hunter," he explained. "The Greeks didn't agree why, but he got put up in the sky after he died." Dad loved the mythology. "The star on the right of his belt, is really two stars," he continued as he lined up the sighting scope. "See?"

I had to adjust the focus for my eyes, but I could see two stars in Orion's belt. It was not as easy to see as the two stars in the Big Dipper, but like all the night sky, we could see things in rural north Nebraska that people in a city could only read about. I wanted to share the stars with Millie.

It had been an odd day, and Mom was so excited she could hardly contain herself. Two days before, she'd gotten up early and driven Dad to Sioux Falls. That was unusual in itself, but he didn't come back with her either. When I asked her where he was, she told me to wait and see. One emergency call had come in yesterday, and she'd told the person that Dad would be back today, but they could call Northern Emergency Services if they wanted faster help.

What was up?

As we were eating lunch, a car, a small sport vehicle as they used to be called, came up the driveway. I noticed right away that it didn't make any noise, and especially there was no surge in sound as it crossed the small gully and came up the last little hill into our yard. It was as though it was being pushed by magic. Dad waved at me through the front window.

The car was an ancient Tesla, one of the early battery cars. This one had been bought by a woman in Omaha, and when she died, her son kept it but didn't use it. When his son inherited it, he had no interest in it and wanted to get rid of it. Dad bought it sight unseen off the Internet. Dad had to buy new tires before he drove home, but it only had about 35,000 miles on it and the finish was old, but not bad.

"It was a find, is all I can say," he bragged. "Now of course, the battery isn't what it was when it was when it was new. I had to stop three times to charge it for eight hours. That was a bummer, but wow! Isn't she beautiful."

Mom walked around and looked at it. "Can we charge it?" she asked nodding toward our solar panels.

"I think we can," said Dad. "It may take a day, but

we'll have to find out." Mom said they'd talked about this car for a long time, but I hadn't known because the conversations had been at bedtime after I was in my room. She was skeptical, but happy that Dad was excited, so she played along.

She turned off the stove, and we all got in the car. "Where to?" asked Dad.

"Let's go to Cy's place," I said.

"Good idea. He'd like this. He'd say the modern world has arrived in rural America."

I noticed the silent glide down the little gully from our yard, but I marveled at the equally silent glide up the similarly gentle hill leading down our road toward the highway. Dad drove carefully on the dirt. "It's got four-wheel drive, but it's a separate motor on each wheel, and I'm not sure how good a shape they're all in."

But on the highway, he pushed the accelerator, and we jerked forward. It was odd because there was no sound of an engine.

He pointed to a gauge on the panel. "That's how much power we have left. This thing hasn't been used for a long time. Part of the day I picked it up I spent finding tires that fit. They're an odd size that isn't used much any more. You should have seen the cracks in the old tires. Scary!"

Dad used the brakes to manage a curve, and I realized how fast we were going, so silently. "The cool part," he said—Dad loved to use ancient slang—"is that when I slow down, the brakes capture energy from our motion and use it to help recharge the battery."

As Cy's last contact in the area, Dad had locked Cy's gate, and he still had the key. He unlocked the gate, and it brought back memories. Cy had never locked his farm. He just casually closed the gate. In theory, someone might have wanted to steal his cows, but stealing cows two at a time across northern Nebraska wouldn't be a profitable crime spree. There were too many people who'd notice a stranger, and too many miles to drive before one was out of the area. Maybe they'd get away if there was a big storm and tornados and everyone was distracted, but otherwise, in rural areas, you can't hide easily unless you have your own hiding place already hidden, so to speak.

I'd not been to Cy's for months since he'd sold the cows. Weeds grew up to his front porch, but the place looked neat. That reflected the fact that Cy kept everything in such good shape that things would hold together without him for a long time. He built things to last.

As we started back, Dad pointed out the gauge, "We've still got about sixty miles or so to go. When we get back, I'll fix up the charger. I think we can run it right off our solar panels. I charged it last night, but that was only about 100 miles out. That's the only problem: You can't go too far on a single charge."

I nodded and enjoyed the ride, but visiting Cy's had made me think about Millie. I sent her an email when we got home, but she never wrote back.

—∿—

Once Dad started driving the Tesla, his pickup sat unused except on the days Mom drove me to school, or on Saturdays when I rode with her to get mail at Lucy's.

Lucy thought the Tesla was a joke. "Hi, Ms Kobb," she smiled. "I know my gas isn't cheap, but it's not so high that the doc needs to go to his panel power."

"Boys and their toys," Mom answered.

"Well at least it's better than chasing women," Lucy said, "but who's there to chase around here anyway?" She and Mom laughed, but I was confused. On the way home, I asked Mom how Dad could chase women. I didn't think he liked to run that much.

She smiled. "It's just a joke that Lucy told. I'll explain some time, but not now. Or you can ask your dad if you want." I took 'if you want' to mean if I dared, and decided to let that sit for now.

—∿—

Dad had in mind for me to learn to drive going around the yard in Mom's car, a Toyota pickup truck with 200,000 miles on it. "It's just getting broken in properly," he claimed and added, "Now that we have a spare car, there is something I can use if you, uh, if we have an accident." He tousled my hair.

His idea of learning to drive was that I should run the truck back and forth in the driveway until I started and stopped very smoothly. "Good start," he said when I thought I'd mastered that. "Now, let's add something." He put a glass of water on the dashboard. "Get back to me when you start and stop and don't spill any."

That was easy with a half a glass, but Dad added water each day until it was just below the rim. And when I had mastered that, he said, "That's really good on flat ground. Now do it down the gully and back."

It took several weeks to get the knack of starting slowly enough and stopping gradually enough not to spill the water. "Good. Now we're ready to drive down to the road." That was about a mile with curves and places to slow down and speed up.

Again, he started me out with half a glass of water, and I graduated up to a full glass. When I could go down and back with a full glass, he said I was ready to drive on the road to Cy's place. I liked driving, but I was sad because I wanted to ask Millie if she was learning to drive too, and she still hadn't written back.

Soon after school started, Dad got a call that Cy had died. That changed my world more than when Martha died. As long as Cy owned the ranch, I assumed he'd be back, and Millie would visit in the summers. "Who's going to be on Cy's farm now?" I asked Dad.

"I don't know, but my guess is it'll probably go to his daughter, Millie's mom. She's their only child." I had a sinking feeling that Dad was right, and also that her mom would never keep the ranch, and I'd never see Millie again.

On Saturday, we drove down to the memorial service for Cy. There were several other ranchers there, including Ronnie's dad. Ronnie didn't come. Millie's dad was there, but he wasn't sitting next to her mom. Instead Millie sat between her parents, and her mom sat next to a man with long dark hair. When everyone stood to go out, Millie held her dad's hand, but her mom took the arm of the man who'd been sitting beside her. I guessed he was The Jerk.

At the reception, Mom and Dad told Millie's mom how sorry they were, and urged her to let them know when she was coming up to the ranch. Millie's mom said something that I couldn't hear.

Millie stood across the room with her dad. She looked defeated, or like she was lost and didn't know where to go. I made a little wave when she saw that I was looking at her, but she looked away and didn't wave back.

We started home after the reception. I sat between Mom and Dad in the front seat of the Toyota. Dad loved his Tesla, but even after he'd tried various ways to run down and recharge the battery, he couldn't get it to go more than about 100 or so miles without stopping to charge it.

I dozed between my parents. They thought I was asleep and started talking. "I bet that was the shock of her life," said Dad.

"Well, I can't see as I blame him," replied Mom.

"It's just going to sit there until she's twenty-one. I guess it won't make much difference. It's not like we need to turn the lights off. Her dad asked me to check on the place for them. I said I would."

"Do you think she'll keep it then?"

"Probably not, but it's not worth much to sell either. Taxes are almost free with the Rural Settlement Plan, so who can predict? She might just let it sit there."

"Yes. Or she might rent it to some idiot who wants to live there."

Mom reached across me and playfully poked Dad in the side.

I must have slept more than I realized because the fragments of conversation were cryptic without context on who was her and who was he.

"... and that guy she's with," said Mom. "Do you think her dad will try for custody?"

"I don't know. He travels so much, it might not be much better."

It was snowing as Dad woke me to go into the house when we got home.

That was the first hard winter I could remember, so cold that no one missed not having a deer season. I kept going to satellite school. There were days that we could not get out for the snow, and Dad struggled to keep both cars running.

The Toyota was better for the snow, especially when it was well below freezing. Other days, he drove the Tesla. Neither one was foolproof, and for both of them there were times he called Horace or Jonathan to pull him out of a ditch with their tractor or to help him start the Toyota from a dead battery. Despite Mom's worries, the Tesla battery didn't die as long as Dad didn't drive it more than an hour from home.

Dad had managed to get only one cow pregnant with his egg technique, although he tried with seven from the area. A lot of ranchers decided to buy semen from the vet school in Omaha. They had Doc Porter put the semen in their cows. That worked about half the time.

There was more talk of trying to do something like that for the deer, but no one ever got around to it.

That fall, I was officially a high school student, a freshman. I couldn't get a real driver's license, but no one would ever check in the country and that was the way that I, and most of my classmates, got to mid-week classes. As long as I didn't drive near cities, the state troopers would leave me alone.

It also meant I could stop to get the mail on the way home. The first time I stopped at Lucy's, she was good-natured. "I miss your mom. Gotta' get her back here. You're cute, but you're boring."

I blushed.

Being a freshman also meant I played on our high school football team. There were only fourteen high school-age guys registered for satellite school and the biweekly classes combined, so not playing wasn't an option. Our community's bragging rights were at stake, and everyone signed up.

I wasn't any better at handling a football than I'd been with a baseball or a basketball, so I'd most likely end up on the line, but that wasn't appealing at all. I was tall, but not bulky, and when I played on the line I'd get clobbered every time. Dad had foreseen this, and for all his avoidance of sports, he realized that I'd be best off if I could learn to be a kicker.

He said he'd played soccer some as a kid, but soccer was too Mexican to catch on in mostly white, rural Nebraska. I wasn't even aware that he'd played any sport, since he'd never brought it up. None of the guys I knew played soccer, and I'd never tried to kick a soccer ball, so we skipped that introductory step and went straight to football.

Dad believed in repetition, and in his mind, the best way to get repetition was to have a lot of balls and keep kicking. So he bought six footballs and six kicking tees and lined them up facing the barn. After I'd kicked all six, he'd pick up the balls, set them up again, and tell me to start over. Sometimes Mom stepped in and helped if Dad had to be gone somewhere.

After a week of just kicking footballs, Dad found some videos on YouTube about how to kick a field goal. "It's really about like a goal kick in soccer. You don't run at the ball headed where you want the ball to go. You run in sideways and swing your foot like a golf club. Wham!" His aim wasn't too good, but Dad still had the power to kick the ball almost over the barn. It was Mom who told me later he'd played soccer in college, but quit during medical school because he couldn't find a team to play with.

I became a specialty kicker, something unheard of in the rural league, but the league itself was changing to adapt to smaller teams. No school had enough students to have eleven-man teams, so they played seven on a side.

With a smaller team they cut the field in half and played only fifty yards, but then someone got the idea for what came to be called half-field football. The field was still 100 yards long, but only twenty-seven yards wide.

This allowed long runs, but there were some special

rules. There had to be four men on the line, a quarterback, and two backs. The four men were always the center, a tackle, and a guard, and an end. The center had to set within five yards of one side or the other of the field. The team with possession could choose for each play.

The other major rule was that the team on defense could not rush between the center and the side of the field, and the team on offense could not pass on that side. The only exception was that a backfield runner—but never the quarterback—could run between the center and the short side of the field. When that happened anyone could run anywhere.

This put long passes back into the game, and it meant the kicks had to be precisely down the middle, and the middle was narrow when you looked at it down the field.

Dad's idea for me to be a kicker paid off. I scored a couple of field goals while other teams without a special kicker almost always missed the goal, and sometimes they missed an extra point after a touchdown. We played teams up to 100 miles away, which gives some idea of how far we had to go to find a team to play and how few people lived in rural Nebraska, at least in our area.

Some of the schools had fields that had been regulation, a full fifty-four yards wide, when the schools were larger to accommodate more students. As people left farms and the rural communities, they changed into playing half-field like the rest of us, but usually they still had two sets of locker rooms like they'd had before. To be sure both facilities were in good shape, the visiting team flipped a coin to see which team got which locker room.

The smaller schools had more primitive facilities, and at one small school, we all shared one locker room. The fathers of the home team had rigged a rope and hung blankets to divide the space. The teams took turns using the showers after the game. We'd won and some of the guys on the other team were still trying to beat us in some way. As we were getting dressed, I stood with my back to the rest of our team as I usually did to hide myself around other guys. It's funny to think back that it never registered with me that all the other guys stood with their back to the center of the room, too.

This time I was in the sort-of corner where the blanket came to the wall. I had dried myself and bent over to put one foot into my underwear when the blanket was ripped back and a player on the other team was standing there in his boxer shorts. "Surprise!" he yelled. We stared eye-to-eye for a moment, and then his eyes shifted to my naked self, and he yelled out, "What the fuck is that?"

I was mortified that he'd seen my hypospadias. Still on one foot, and not wanting to trip myself on my underwear, I hopped to turn to face my teammates who were all staring at me, too. But I had one hand over my penis as I held the waist of my underwear, and the other hand held out the side of my underwear as I hopped to get my second foot through its leg hole. My team did not see me. The player on the other team turned to his teammates. "What a freak. Fuck! What a freak!"

Their coach was in the room now. "Break it up. Nichols, was that you again? What have I told you about sportsmanship?"

Meanwhile, I managed to get my second foot through the leg hole and pull up my underwear. Quickly I pulled on my jeans and was out the door on our side.

One of my teammates followed me out and asked, "What's the hair up his ass?" I kept my answer simple to avoid getting tripped up by anything I said, "No idea."

Mom was waiting with the other parents. Dad had not been able to come to this game. "What was the yelling about?" she asked.

"Oh, just some pervert asshole on the other team," I tried to sound nonchalant.

That was the first time I'd ever sworn in front of Mom, and she looked deeply at my face like if she looked hard enough she'd see beyond the lie I'd just told her.

High school meant parties. At first I heard rumors, more

accurately a few comments on the days that we had class in the early part of the week. But after I'd scored some field goals I was more accepted, and I started being told where parties would be.

These weren't at someone's home or at school or something planned with parents. They were gatherings of kids at sites determined in some group process I never understood. The whole thing reminded me of the selection of a campsite when the dads used to go camping to start deer season.

There was always booze, usually beer purchased by some kid's dad, sometimes wine, and rarely rum and Coke or the like. Sometimes someone would share some marijuana, but that was not usual for group parties. People wanted to get boisterous, and "Mary Jane," as my dad referred to it, often left guys too mellow.

My parents resisted letting me take one of our cars. That meant that I couldn't join the groups. I begged them to let me use a car, until Ronnie offered to pick me up out at the road. I'd need to walk the mile, but it was worth it to me.

That tipped the balance. Mom didn't want me riding with Ronnie, so she persuaded Dad to let me drive the Toyota.

There were shouts of "Hey, Kobb," and "Look who's here. Hi, Jack," when I arrived, but I held back and watched. My parents didn't drink or use drugs. Not because of any strong belief but because they just didn't like them. Dad said one time, "I've never had a wine that was a good trade-off for how I felt the next day."

But it was hard not to have a drink, and that created its own problems. I'd never had a drink before. It wasn't the first one that was a problem, but rather the fact that after having had one drink I had no perception of what a second drink would do to me. As I got lazily drunk, my new friends—the sophomores, juniors, and seniors—laughed with me, before they laughed at me. And all that time, I didn't know where I was heading, only that my judgment wasn't great.

I've learned in just a few years that there are different kinds of drunks. There are angry drunks. There are laughing drunks. There are quiet drunks. I'm the last kind. I just got quieter and quieter. Finally a girl named Betty sat beside me and put her hand on my shoulder. She was two years older than me, a junior. "You're kind of cute, Kobb," she said. I rubbed my shoulder against her hand and leaned toward her.

Betty stood up, took my hand, and got me to sit beside her on a log where we could watch everyone else. Guys were singing songs that I guess had been sung by drunks for ages. Most of them were stories in some way or another about boys and girls. I didn't understand most of what they said, but I joined in, and Betty watched me.

"Twas a cold winter's evening

The guests were all leaving,

O'Leary was closing the bar ..." and so on.

Some guy laughed, and I started to laugh.

Betty put her hand on my chin and turned my face toward her. She started to kiss me, when I felt a sudden tightening of my stomach and I burped. When she pulled back to look at me, I vomited.

Betty side-jumped out of the way, but I threw up on my shoes and lost my balance. As I tried to keep from falling forward, I overreacted and fell backwards. "Guess Kobb's had his limit," someone said.

I fell asleep, and woke up perhaps an hour later when Betty shook me. "Come on, Kobb. Let's get you cleaned up." She wiped my chin and nose with tissues from her backpack. I doubt I was the only person who ever got sick at a party, but I was definitely the most recent one.

Betty drove my dad's car, and the friend who'd brought her followed us. She drove up our dirt road until, just before the gully, she pulled to the side and stopped. "Here's the key. Tell your parents in the morning that you got stuck or something, so you left the car here. Let's go." With that, she walked with me across the gully and watched me until I got in the house.

I got into bed quietly. In the morning I could smell my clothes, so I washed them in the bathroom sink before I went to breakfast. I wasn't hungry anyway, and my head hurt so much that rinsing out my shirt was all I could manage.

I tried to thank Betty at school the next week, but she was with some other girls and one of them made a wisecrack about bringing a puke bag to the next party. There are no secrets in small schools.

About a month later when I got home from school, Mom greeted me saying, "You missed all the excitement."

"What was that?"

"Dad saw smoke from Cy's farm and thought it was on fire. Turns out there's a man renting the place." That was unexpected, since there was hardly anyone who'd move to our area.

"His name is Edwards," Dad explained when he got back from making a house call. "He's rented it for two years. It's not real clear what he plans to do." Dad had seen smoke from the north road. He got suspicious as soon as he found the gate wasn't locked because he thought he had the only key. The man explained he got a key from the person who rented to him on behalf of Cy's family. It all fit together, but Dad was still puzzled. Why hadn't he been told Edwards was coming?

"He was polite, but you'd have thought I caught him with his pants down, coming up the road without him expecting me. Of course he understood right away why I was there, since I was watching the place.

"The smoke was from burning weeds so that made

sense. He said he was going to raise some cattle, but he wasn't like any farmer I've ever seen. I kept wondering what he wasn't saying." Dad paused to think out loud. "His fingernails were way too clean."

The next Saturday, I borrowed Dad's field glasses and went to the hill between the creek bed and Cy's barn. I could see the house, the barn, and the open place where Mr. Edwards had parked his pickup. There was no one to see for a long time. Then Mr. Edwards walked from the house to the barn carrying a box that he left there. He went back into the house, and I waited an hour at least before I finally gave up and went back home to eat lunch.

I wondered who this guy was. He wore jeans that were faded like most of us. Lace-up boots, not pull up like a typical rancher, but some of the guys at school wore lace-up boots, too. So that wasn't odd. His pickup was splashed along the side where he'd driven through mud and not cleaned it off.

But Dad had mentioned that Mr. Edward's fingernails were way too clean, and I decided I was going to watch him for awhile.

I went to one more party but didn't drink. I couldn't get into the mood of things because I was afraid to repeat what'd happened before. I sat with Betty, but it was awkward. Another time, I tried to talk to her at school, but she didn't say much. I tried to make conversation until she left me sitting by myself and walked away with one of her friends.

That was enough to make me an outsider. Guys forgot to tell me where to find the gang on Friday nights. I learned quickly how long's the time from Friday afternoon to Monday morning if the only people you see are your parents.

After parties, the guys still bragged at class breaks the next week about what they'd done over the weekend, what they got away with, trying to kiss or touch one of the girls. "Yeah, I had my hand on her breast," or "The skin of her ass was so smooth." These things were usually said in a way to make what they were talking about sound great and to imply that everyone else was losing out. Some of the senior guys talked about how to "do it." They bragged like experts, and I was impressed at the time. More than I would ever be now.

The bragging always ran into a reality check. No matter how you looked at it, and no matter how much a guy said, it was a very small community, and there were no safe secrets. Besides making out, sex was limited to kissing and fondling.

The guy who bragged the most knew he didn't need to worry about getting a girl pregnant. "My dad says he had to worry that a girl might get knocked up," he said with authority, "but it's simpler for us. A girl has to go along with it to get pregnant these days, so we can do anything we can, and never have to worry."

The same guy talked about how if a girl wanted to have a baby, she'd give some doctor her egg and he'd get semen from a guy and put them together. I thought of Dad and the bulls, and I had a vague memory of what I saw when I walked in on Mom and Dad before she assigned me to use my own bathroom. Whatever was happening, I assumed that someday it would all make sense, maybe when I was a senior myself. Until then, I hid my hypospadias and tried to blend in as much as I could.

To pass the weekends I created a project for myself: determining what Mr. Edwards was up to. Days when I didn't have to drive to school, after I finished my chores, I'd take Dad's binoculars and a jug of water and go sit on the hill to watch Cy's place, but there wasn't much to see. Most of the time the new guy was in the house. I knew he was there because he'd go to the barn or his car to put something in it or take something out, but that would take only a couple of minutes out of a couple of hours.

I was about to abandon my efforts until one morning I went over early before I'd done my chores. The sun was still coming up, and Mr. Edwards came out of the house carrying a paper bag and walked to where part of an old fence was attached to a corner of the barn. He pulled out some cans and lined them up on the fence. Then, as he walked back toward the house, he suddenly turned, dropped to one knee and pulled out a pistol from somewhere and held it toward the cans with two hands. The pistol snapped or popped more than it banged as he fired six shots in a row, hitting the next can each time until all of them had been blown away. My mouth hung open, and the field glasses dropped from my eyes. I couldn't believe what I'd seen.

Next he made a motion that I recognized from movies as putting a new clip into the pistol and walked back to retrieve the cans and set them up again. I lifted the field glasses up to watch him more closely and saw that each can had many bullet holes from being used as a target before.

He did this six or seven times. His skill was very different from the skills of the dads who went deer hunting. He hit every can with one shot, never missing, until they were all gone. Then he put the cans back and did it again.

I was up early enough the next Saturday that I was on the hill when he came out of the house. But this time he put the cans on a log that was close to my hill, so that he'd shoot toward me. I panicked. He was a good shot, but I still didn't want him shooting toward me. What if he shot wide and the bullet came toward me?

There'd be no time to duck. Should I shout out, or should I move?

Mr. Edwards stepped back and looked at the cans. He took his pistol from its holster and pointed it toward the cans, and toward me, but it wasn't like before. He turned the gun in his hand like he was inspecting it or checking something. He turned toward the house, and I expected him to turn and start shooting. But just when I thought he'd gone far enough he had to shoot, he put his pistol back in its holster, gathered the cans in the same bag, and took them over and set them up where he always put them.

Then he walked toward the house, abruptly spun and dropped to a knee, and shot all six cans in a row. As he put a new clip in the pistol, he yelled, "My name's Ted. What's yours?"

My heart was racing, and I wished I'd left when he stopped aiming the gun in my direction. "I won't hurt you," he called. "But it's pretty silly to be sitting up in those rocks. It get's hot doesn't it?"

I wasn't sure whether to hide, still hoping he'd decide he really hadn't seen me, or to call back to him, or to stand up. I worried he'd take a shot at me if I stood up, and I knew he wouldn't miss. After a few moments, he called, "I'm going to have a soda. Do you want one?"

That reassured me, and I stood up. He, Ted as he introduced himself, put his gun away and watched me walk down to the farmyard.

"What's your name?" he asked.

"Jack Kobb."

He held out his hand. "Ted Edwards." I shook his hand liked my dad had taught me. "Pleased to meet you Mr. Edwards."

"Jeeze, you make me feel ancient with the 'mister' stuff. Call me Ted."

"My mom won't let me call an adult by his first name."

"Okay, I'll be Mr. Edwards if I ever meet your parents. But this is my place. Call me Ted here. House rules. You related to Percy Kobb?"

"My dad."

"Nice guy. We met a few weeks ago, but he seems pretty busy and hasn't been back." He took a deep breath like he wanted to act friendly but had other things on his mind. "So Jack, I'll get that soda." He went inside and brought out two glasses with ice and two sodas, one orange and one Coke. He held the cans up in one hand, "You're company. You get first choice."

I took the orange soda and poured it over the ice.

I dreaded summer vacation. Millie didn't visit. Ronnie worked with his dad and besides, it was always awkward since the episode with Charles. Meeting Ted changed all that. Going over to hang out with him wasn't like being a friend with Millie, but Ted was a lot younger than my dad so it was more casual.

The best part was that Ted taught me to shoot a gun. Not that Dad was opposed to guns. It was more like he felt about team sports. Dad hadn't taught me about team sports because he didn't know how to play them himself. And he'd never learned to shoot a gun because he had a very long list of other things he wanted to do first.

I didn't naturally blend with a gun, becoming one with the weapon like I'd seen Ted do when he shot his pistol. Instead, I tested every bit of his patience. He began by giving me a booklet on gun safety. "Read it cover to cover and be ready to answer questions." That completed our first lesson. The booklet wasn't long, and I read it quickly after dinner.

The next day, before he even said hello, Ted asked, "Kobb, what are the parts of a cartridge?"

"Uh …"

"Bullet! Case! Primer! Propellant! What is the first rule of gun safety?"

"Be careful?"

"Number one, treat all guns as if they are loaded." He wasn't angry. In fact, I never saw Ted angry this or any other time, but he was making his point. "Don't read the book, Kobb. Study it. Memorize it. What's in it can save your life or the life of someone you love."

"Yes, sir." I didn't know where the sir came from, but it seemed to fit the moment.

We killed time doing other things, but we didn't do

anything more with gun lessons that day. I went home and read the book like my life depended on it, and did much better with questions the next day. I also asked Ted how he was such a good shot.

"My dad taught me. And I was an MP in the army. Lots of practice." Then he told me that he'd decided he'd teach me first on a rifle. He owned a high-power hunting rifle, but he had me start on a 0.22 with a five-cartridge magazine.

He stood beside me with his hunting rifle and had me copy with the 0.22 exactly what he did in each step.

"Do you hunt deer?" I asked because it was a rifle like some of the dads had.

"No. Brought it for coyotes."

"There hasn't been a coyote around her since I can remember. The ranchers killed most with guns and poisoned the last ones."

"Then I was misinformed, I guess."

Just after the Fourth of July, Ted took off for a week. When he came back, he brought two calves. He'd already heard that was the maximum you could support on the amount of water he'd have left after he took care of his own needs. He might have been able to do three since it was only him and there was no one else using water to drink and stuff, but he stuck with the local wisdom.

Doc Porter came over and worked their vaccinations. One was a young bull, and Doc said, "I can make him a steer, but we've not been doing that around here."

"Why not?" Ted asked.

"Guess you've been off the farm too long to have heard, but there's problems breeding cattle and around here anyways, we're keeping all our options open to us."

Ted took Doc's advice. The calves settled into their new home in his barn. Most of the repairs had been completed after Cy moved to Omaha, but the wood hadn't been painted. "Annoys me it's so unfinished. You want to help me fix that?"

I briefly thought of the joke on the painters in the novel Tom Sawyer and his fence, but it sounded like something to try once. The city rancher who'd built our place put on what looked like shingle siding, but when you got close to it, it was fiberglass sections so it wouldn't burn. So Dad never had to paint our house.

Mom and Dad started talking that summer about what I'd do after I finished high school in two years. None of the guys I knew planned to go to college, and I wasn't sure I wanted to keep going to school. Mom and Dad, however, thought college was a good idea. "You may want to stay here," Dad said, "but you may eventually find that you're tired of this place. Going to college gives you choices. Choices are the key."

In a young boy's way, I'd begun to assume I'd be a doctor like Dad and Kobb, but I had no real idea what that meant. I knew my dad as a person who gave shots, held hands and ran to emergencies. He never talked about the physics, organic chemistry, and molecular biology that came first.

Mom got on the Internet to look for advice and found that the satellite school system had counselors who'd talk to us about college. We could make an appointment for a counselor to visit us at home, but there weren't but a couple of counselors for the whole of rural Nebraska, so we'd have had to get on a list and they only traveled on Fridays. The rest of the time they had office hours in Omaha Monday through Thursday.

Mom wasn't the kind who liked to wait once she'd made up her mind, so she made an appointment for a Tuesday morning in August. We were going to come down to Omaha the night before, so I wrote to Millie to ask if she and I could have ice cream or something either the night we were there or after my appointment. She wrote back that she'd meet me for ice cream at lunchtime at the same cafe near her home.

The counseling session opened new ideas for me. I got excited at the idea of being in a place with a lot of kids my own age, but it was also a bit scary. The counselor had me take a test that asked stuff like whether I liked crowds or small groups. I answered crowds, and she assumed I was comfortable around a lot of people. But the reason I marked crowds was that I hoped I could stay to the side and no one would expect anything from me.

Whatever I chose to do, I'd need to come back down on a separate trip to take a test in a secure testing center. The counselor explained how I'd sign in, and then check everything I had—cell phone, lunch, jacket, etc.—in a locker before I entered a room with about a hundred computers. There wasn't a testing center any closer than coming back down to Omaha in the fall.

After the appointment, I texted Millie that we were on our way to the cafe. We got there and waited over two hours, but she didn't show up. I texted her again, but she never texted me back.

I didn't plan on telling anyone why I was going to Omaha, but our team missed one of our games because of bus trouble, and it was rescheduled for the weekend I was to go. That led to some grief from the guys because I had to explain why I couldn't reschedule the trip to make it to the game. They appreciated my kicking, but the teasing about college was brutal. "So the big scholar is too important for us ..." and "If you can't make it as a real man, go hide in school." Others were simply angry. "Why is your stupid exam more important than our team?"

And with that I was an outsider again.

I was fifteen on my last birthday, so this time I had an official learner's permit and with Mom in the car, I drove the whole way down. We went part way on the two-lane road, but the last hour or so was on the interstate. The divided highway seemed quaintly antiquated—it had been laid out over 100 years before—but there were sections that had been widened and repaved. This was my first time driving on a truly modern road. I loved it.

As we entered the metropolitan area, Mom directed me using her cell phone maps, and we easily found our motel. Omaha was her city, and although the suburbs stretched miles farther out than when she was a girl, the central areas were pretty much as she had known them, with a few exceptions for some new schools, office centers, and stores. Some of her favorites had been taken down, and a couple of times she started a sentence, "See that building? When I was your age that was ..." She'd name a theater, a drive-in, a bookstore, or something else.

We changed as soon as we checked in, because we were going to a play that Millie was in at school. I was still bothered that Millie hadn't shown up at the ice cream parlor a couple of months before, but Mom urged me to give her another chance. "You never know what's really going on for anybody." So we went to the play, and what a play it was! It was set in camps of the American Civil War a couple hundred years ago. Mom had taught me to try to discern the theme in plays and music. The theme here centered on what a person, in this case a woman, would do for love.

Millie played the lead role of a woman whose lover is drafted. She wants to be near him, so she cuts her hair really short, puts on a tight undershirt and a baggy shirt over it, and passes herself off as a young man who plays a drum for the soldiers when they march into battle. You can see where that's headed, and yes, she did get shot, but she survived. They said it was based on a true story. Given that I'd learned in school that women had been fighting in the army for almost 100 years, it was sometimes hard to relate to the issue of women being left at home.

The surprising thing was how convincingly Millie could look like a boy when she tucked her hair into a very short wig, and squeezed her breasts flat. Part of it was the dark makeup that made her look like she needed to shave.

The next morning I had a follow-up appointment with the ophthalmologist, Dad's friend, Dr. Friend. I loved his name. He was very friendly and chatted away as he had me read lines lower and lower on an eye chart, all the way to the bottom.

"You're still quite farsighted," he summed up speaking

as much to me as to my mom in the corner. "But you're young enough I suspect you can see most anything. Except, when you get tired, or try to look real close, glasses will help a lot."

As he entered my new prescription in the computer, a nurse knocked and looked in. "Dr. Friend, there's a doctor on the phone who says it's an emergency and asked me to interrupt you. He said you'd know what it's about."

"Okay." He nodded to her and said to us, "I'll be just a minute. I think I know what this is. It shouldn't take long."

He forgot to close the screen of my record when he stepped out so I peeked when Mom started reading her magazine. A lot of the information was specific doctor type records, but one thing stuck out to me. In a place labeled "Other Health Issues," he had written one phrase, "Small hypospadias," with an exclamation point.

I interpreted that to mean that I not only had hypospadias, my penis was small enough to make a note of it

Friday night, we went to Millie's high school football game. I was excited because I'd never seen a full-field football game. With a bigger field came a bigger crowd, concession stands instead of homemade cookies, and lights. They got to play under the lights.

We sat with Millie's mom and her boyfriend. I could

only think of how Millie always called him The Jerk. The funny thing was that his real name was very similar, something like Dirk, and when I was introduced I almost said, "Pleased to meet you, Mr. Jerk."

He talked about how good it was of us to visit, especially after Cy's death. "Millie's such a wonderful young girl," he said. "We're all so glad she's in our lives."

Millie was part of a group of pom-pom girls who danced crazy sexy on the sidelines. Even on the cool night, their uniforms were at the most four inches high on the top and four inches high on the bottom. At least their shoes covered their feet.

I wasn't used to seeing girls, really women in every way except their age, move their bodies that way. It was like an invitation and taunting at the same time, especially when they looked away and bent forward or looked toward the stands and bent forward, with their hair falling over their faces, to emphasize their butts or their breasts.

Mom had us go back to our motel after the game so I'd get a good night's sleep before my tests the next day.

I took tests all day Saturday. The monitors were so concerned about cheating that I had to register with my thumbprint on a scanner at the desk and confirm my thumbprint on another scanner by the computer I used to take the test. They matched both of them with the thumbprint I'd given to the Department of Motor

Vehicles when I got my driving learner's permit.

There was a section on mathematics, a section on grammar and reading skills, and a section on ethics. They provided a calculator for the math section. You couldn't use your own because they worried someone would figure out how to put formulas on their calculator or cheat in some other way. Dad had told me about the subjects and rules in advance.

The ethics questions were a recent addition. The idea was that higher education carried some responsibility, but just as for the rest of the test, someone could read and study enough to guess the right answers. I think they figured asking the questions discouraged some cheating, even if a person didn't really believe any of the human rights and equality stuff.

Millie took me to a party that night. She was my introduction, and she did watch out for me, but I was as much an outsider as I'd been at parties at home. She drank with everyone else. I held and sipped a single beer. I knew I'd be spending the night in the motel room with Mom. She'd tolerate it if I smelled a little like alcohol, but she'd be upset if I was drunk. Besides, it was a long drive home in the morning, and I didn't want to be hung over like the time with kids near home.

I told Millie that we'd sat with her mom and The

Jerk at the game. “The bastard,” she said. “He pretends to be so nice in front of Mom, but when she’s not looking, he touches me.” This was outside of my experience or even any story I’d ever heard. “At first, he’d act like it was accidental, and excuse himself and say he was sorry. After the fourth or fifth time, I didn’t buy that, and I’d just stare. Once he knew there was no way he was fooling me, he just touched me any time Mom wasn’t looking.”

“Have you told your mom?” I asked because that was the only way I could think to help her.

“Yeah,” Millie said and rolled her eyes like I was naive even to suggest that. “But when she confronted him, he said it was my fault. That I knew I’d never have a real man from boys my age, and I was trying to compensate. And that’s how it is …”

Millie realized she’d said more than she planned to, and abruptly went back into the party and introduced me to one of the football players. He shook my hand, or more accurately crushed my hand, sort of a territorial thing I think in retrospect. But there was no reason for him to worry about me. Millie circulated with her friends, chugging a drink here and there, while I drifted to the corner where I became an unnoticed observer. I watched how she danced with her football player, put her hands on his waist, and then tucked her fingers inside the waist of his jeans.

A friend of hers, a girl, sought me out, "You're the guy who lives next to Millie's ranch, aren't you?"

"Where her grandfather lived, yes."

"It's not hers now?"

"I don't know." Suddenly I was an outsider, unaware even of what was happening in my own neighborhood.

"Let's dance," said Millie's friend. I hesitated, but let her lead me by the hand to the open area where everyone was moving in unison. My moves were subtle—well, actually so subtle that no one could see anything except my shoulders moving up and down ever so slightly with the music.

The center of the room opened up, and a group of girls, led by Millie, started dancing with their arms in the air and their bodies swaying with the music. Her dress lifted with her arms. For a moment I thought she wasn't wearing underwear. Everyone else formed a crowd around them, several people deep, and clapped.

The rhythm sped up. They all danced faster, especially Millie. She both led the group and hid in it. Then she stepped to my side of the circle, reached past two people in front of me, grabbed my hand and pulled me in. She was lost in the music.

I felt like a mutant on display. I couldn't keep up with her, and mercifully she pulled her football player into the circle. He danced with her, with his hands on her shoulders, then her waist, and then lifting the hem of her skirt.

It rarely snowed in Nebraska anymore, so Christmas was cooler but not cold. One of Mom's friends drove to Sioux Falls and brought back several turkeys. On Christmas day, several women cooked turkeys in their own kitchens and brought them to our house for a kind of community dinner. Being built for many guests, our house was the natural place to gather, even though we only had a small table. A lot of folks brought camp tables and stools to sit on.

Ted was invited, along with Ronnie and his parents, the families who'd gone deer hunting, and those who played football. Between all of those groups, everyone for fifty miles was invited. Since the weather was dry, it wasn't over an hour's drive for anyone.

"We used to drive that long to get across Omaha sometimes," Dad told me. We'd been up early with the animals and then getting the dinner ready, so we didn't exchange presents until late in the evening after everyone had left.

I had a small present each for Mom and Dad. They exchanged presents and then Dad gave me a large box. "It's from both of us," he said. I shook the box but had no idea what was in it as I pulled off the paper. Then I was shocked. The box said "Remington" on the outside. It was my own 0.22 caliber rifle, with a five-shot magazine.

"Mr. Edwards helped me pick it out," Dad said. "I don't know anything about guns, but I know you've had fun learning to shoot."

"Thank you." I hugged them both. "Thank you."

Kobb showed up New Year's Eve afternoon. "Thought I'd bring in the New Year with you," he said. I showed him my new rifle, and we went out and set some cans on a stump, so we'd shoot with the hill as a backstop.

I shot first and hit a couple of cans, but missed most. Kobb was a very good shot. He hit four cans with five shots.

"Where'd you learn to shoot like that?" I asked.

"With friends," he said.

"Did you ever teach Dad to shoot?"

"No. Your grandmother didn't like guns." He changed the subject. "So Jack, a fine young man like you, have you got a girlfriend?"

I thought of Millie, but that thought was immediately crowded out by the memory of her and the football player. "Not really ..."

"Huh," he grunted. "What about Cy's granddaughter? You seemed to like her I heard."

I looked toward where Mom was watching us from the house to figure out how Kobb knew about Millie. "Well, I sort of like this girl, but I think she's got a boyfriend."

"That's not an obstacle," he said. "You don't know how I met your grandmother, do you?"

"No."

"Well, it's like this." Kobb took a big breath and started talking like he was telling a long joke. "So, this man gets off a motorcycle after a really long ride. He's been riding for days. Something has gone horribly wrong. He's lost everyone he ever cared about. And he goes into a bar, and a guy at the next table wants to talk, but the motorcycle rider only wants to drink his beer." He paused. "You sure you haven't heard this before?" I shook my head no.

"Okay," Kobb said, and then he continued. "Now the motorcycle rider is trying to ignore the other guy, but not make him angry either. When in walks a gorgeous, graceful, tall blonde, and she walks toward the rider. The rider nods to the other guy like to tell him to shut up because she's who he was waiting for.

"But she walks past him and sits with a guy at the next table. The guy who'd been trying to talk to the rider sneers and turns away. But the rider can't take his eyes off the tall blonde.

"Then the guy the girl was meeting gets a call on his cell phone and gets up to talk outside in private. The motorcycle rider, on an impulse he can never explain, gets up and asks the bartender for a piece of paper. He writes a note and goes over and hands it to the girl and walks out.

"The note says, 'I'm going to get my bike. I'll be outside the back door in about five minutes. Pretend you're going to the ladies' room. Meet me out back, and you'll never regret it.' So the rider gets his motorcycle, all the time wondering what the girl will do, and he rides up to the back door. And the girl steps out. He takes off his helmet and gives it to her." Kobb paused for effect, "And your dad was born ten months later."

He left before sunrise on New Year's Day. I practiced shooting until I'd gone through the whole box of bullets Dad had given me with the rifle. In the afternoon, I walked over to Ted's place. He was coming out of the barn and invited me in for hot chocolate. That was pretty unusual because we always talked in the barn or outside.

"Did I hear a motorcycle at your place last night? You know how sound travels at night."

"Yeah. That was my grandfather."

"Oh. I wasn't imagining things then?"

"No. He just shows up sometimes."

"Is he still there?"

"No, he left real early this morning."

"Short visit. He visit often?"

"Not really. Maybe every year or so."

"Where's he live the rest of the time?"

"I don't know. I don't think Dad does either. He did say he'd be back for my birthday this summer. I'll be sixteen."

"That's good. He's a doctor too, isn't he?"

"Used to be. Not any more."

The day after school ended for the summer, Mom got a secure ePDF message from Millie's mom asking if Millie could visit us for a month.

I felt bad after the party in Omaha in the fall, and Kobb's questions about a girlfriend had made me feel inadequate, so I wished Millie's mom hadn't asked in the first place. But I couldn't say that to Mom. I told her it was okay with me.

Dad let me drive the Tesla up to South Dakota to pick Millie up in Sioux Falls. Sioux Falls was on the interstate so even though they had lost most local businesses since the drought, there was enough through traffic to keep it alive, and it had bus service. Because the battery pack in the Tesla was so old, I had to plan on a recharge before we drove back.

I figured that Millie had left Omaha at the latest by 6:00 a.m. and maybe earlier since I was picking her up at noon.

She was different, even since the fall in Omaha. When

I first saw her, I thought she was a boy, and I kept looking for who else had gotten off the bus until she pulled my sleeve and said "Hi." She was dressed like when she played the part in her play at school. Her hair was cut short and dyed black as motor oil, and shiny that way, too. All she carried was a backpack. She wore a loose shirt, and I wondered why her breasts didn't show at all. The perfect touch was that she'd put faint dark makeup on her chin, so her face suggested a boy who hadn't shaved for a day or so.

I cared for her more than anyone, maybe even more than my mom, but it was difficult to connect the dots that this person was the same as the girl I'd splashed in the water with when we were kids.

On the drive back, she asked me to put on what she called music. It had long notes, like the recordings of whales before the Japanese hunters killed so many under the pretext of research that they died off completely. Except the whale sounds were low and deep, while these were more of a screech, like a person learning to play a violin. It hurt to listen to the sound, but Millie seemed to be trying to express something by asking me to listen to it. It was up to me to try to get the message, but I didn't.

We didn't say more than a couple of words while we waited an hour at the charging station. Millie just looked around nervously. I wondered if she was checking me out, comparing me to her football player, perhaps laughing at my awkward anxiousness to make a good impression even though I'd known her for years. She was tense and ready to jump, and once we were on the road, and you could see for miles that there was nobody else there, she was still anxious.

Mom was oblivious to any of this when we arrived home just before sunset. She welcomed Millie and gave her a big hug like a long lost child. "I put you in the bedroom that connects to Jack's room," she said to her. "It won't be a problem sharing the bathroom, will it?"

I almost laughed out loud. Mom missed that she was putting a very mature teenager next to her very inexperienced, almost naive, son.

I hadn't been around many girls since I made a fool of myself with Betty, but that didn't mean I missed that Millie's breasts had grown a lot since the fall, or at least they were more obvious once she put on a regular shirt. It could have been that she seemed happier then, and that she'd worn a bulky sweater in the car, but now she wore a tight top with a deeply scooped neck. She was clothed, but she was clothed in a way that left little to the imagination.

We sat on the porch and chatted after dinner. Small stuff. Her mom was looking after her cat. We didn't have a horse to ride right now. Nobody rode horses any more. They needed too much water. It got cold after the sun went down, and she sneezed.

"I got up really early. It's getting cold," she said. "Can I just go to bed?"

"Sure. No problem," I replied.

I stayed downstairs and helped Mom finish laying out dishes and silverware for breakfast. We were celebrating Millie's visit with pancakes, and Mom had read a recipe one time that said it was better if the batter was made the night before. I measured the flour and other dry ingredients while she cracked eggs and melted butter. We had pancakes down to a ritual.

Millie's light was off when I came upstairs. I slipped off my jeans and brushed my teeth. Knowing that she might have heard me made me think of Kobb teaching me how to pee standing up. I turned off the light before I closed the door and returned to my room.

I didn't hear any sound from her side of the door, but as soon as I turned off the light by my bed, the door to the bathroom opened a crack. It was Millie. "Can I come in?" she asked.

"Sure," I answered.

There was no light to see her by. In the country there is no distant glow from streetlights to keep things from being totally dark. She stumbled briefly on my chair, but did not fall, as she came across the room. Then she was at the side of my bed and she pulled the cover back and lay down next to me. She wasn't naked, but her nightgown was thin and short. I felt myself respond, but I stayed flat on my back. I didn't want to scare her off, and I didn't want to embarrass myself.

She found my arm and lifted it so that she could lie next to my body and then she pulled my arm around her like a shawl over her shoulder. At first I thought it was sexy, but she wasn't looking for sex or even teasing me. "Dad left and went to Albany." She talked to the room more than to me. "They're divorced, and she just married The Jerk. That's why they don't want me around to spoil their little party."

She stopped talking and pulled my hand around her shoulder so that I held her closer, under my arm. And she went to sleep.

The cutout stars my dad had helped me used to make constellations on the ceiling were still glowing. I stared at the patterns until the light from the stars faded, and I fell asleep. When I woke up at first light, Millie had gone back to her room and the door to the bathroom was closed behind her.

In the morning, I dressed and went down to help Mom and Dad fix breakfast. Millie was already there, watching pancakes bubble before she flipped them. She was wearing flannel pajamas buttoned up around her neck.

"I'll have one for you in a minute," she said.

I took a cup of coffee and sat down at the table. In just a minute or so, she set down a perfect letter "J" shaped pancake. "I learned how," she said smiling at me.

I had no idea what was happening, but I knew something had changed. One of us had been hit by a truck or a falling rock—or something.

We relaxed most of that day. I had chores to take care of the chickens and look in on the cows, at least the one that had calved late and was still suckling the calf. There was always something.

Most days when I wasn't having classes with Mom, I'd ride along as Dad made house calls and checked on the cattle of other ranchers, but since Millie was there, I stayed around our farm after I'd done my chores. Millie sat on the shady side of the porch and read. When I came to the house for lunch, I asked, "What you reading?"

"Anna Karenina."

"That's old, isn't it?"

"Yeah, but it's timeless too."

"What do you mean?"

She looked at me in a way that suddenly reminded me of her coming into my room so that I would hold her closely. Again, I didn't understand the message.

"It's all in the first sentence," she said, and then she quoted, "All happy families are alike. Each unhappy family is unhappy in its own way." She looked up at me with a mischievous smile and asked, "What's the system in your misery?"

I paused for a moment to think about what she had asked me, and while I did, she jumped up and went inside to help my mom set the table for lunch.

A couple of days later, we got up at 4:00 a.m. to do our chores early so we could drive to Valentine for the Fourth of July parade and fireworks. We were far enough north that you really noticed the long days in summer, and this was just after what my mom said her Swedish relatives called Midsummer when it never got fully dark.

There was still lunch to prepare, but Mom, Dad and I took care to be quiet so that Millie could sleep the extra hour while we prepared to leave the ranch for a full two days. I left extra feed with the chickens, and I checked the timer on the water pump for the cows. It wasn't predicted to be that hot, but it was always dry.

Millie must have heard us anyway. She came downstairs wearing a really short pair of jean shorts, short enough that the pockets came out down her legs. It was a contrast with the high-necked, buttoned pajamas, but it seemed they could have been from the same set of clothes as her initial nightgown.

We arrived in Valentine about ten o'clock, just as the parade began. This one was mostly kids from ranches all over northwest Nebraska, a few sheriff's deputies on motorcycles, and the small group of kids from Valentine High School that was called the local marching band. There was even a pair of old guys riding horses. The animals weren't very healthy and seemed to struggle even in the moderate heat, but everyone was enthusiastic. Parades or events of any kind were a local highpoint and offered a break from the other challenges of living in a region that was just a ghost of what it had been before the weather change became the usual weather.

This year someone had set up an antique Ferris wheel. It was like opening a curtain to see Valentine unfold as we rode to the top. When we stopped so another couple could get on at the bottom, Millie touched my knee and said, "You're such a good friend. Why do you like me at all?"

I hesitated and then said the first thing that came to my mind, "Because I've known you for a long, long time."

"You've had your cow longer than you've known me. Does that make her a better friend?"

"No. That's not what I mean ..."

She cut me off. "You don't know what you mean, and if you knew me, would you still be my friend? I don't think so."

Just then the Ferris wheel lurched and we descended back into the crowd before coming back around to the top. Only this time we didn't stop, and we'd have had to be sitting still to continue that conversation. The shifting view of the same crowd was too distracting, and Millie changed the conversation to point out things we could see.

Dad talked with the one surgeon at the Valentine Hospital. Mom sold wild herbs that she had gathered and dried. There were cookies, brownies, and pieces of cake and pie on tables by the field. I asked the woman selling the brownies why they were so expensive.

"They're real chocolate. Not that artificial stuff most people use."

"Oh. Where do you get it?" It did have a unique flavor, and I smiled when I tasted it.

"I get it from a man who travels to South America to buy it. He roasts the beans and grinds them himself. He says it takes a couple of days to grind it right."

"Hey, Millie," a voice interrupted us. I looked around, and Charlie was standing beside us staring at Millie's legs and the bottom of her shorts. He ignored my presence and put his arm around her shoulder. "Good to have you with us again. Long time, no see."

Millie didn't answer.

Charlie noticed her lack of response but added, "Well, when you get tired of hanging around with Kobb, here, I'll be around ..." He left us still eating the last of our brownies.

She held up her middle finger as he swaggered away.

There were a few horse-riding competitions in the afternoon. Cattle were too valuable to have the old-time event of steer riding any more. We needed what we had, and there were no cattle to spare or even to risk. What everyone looked forward to was the barbecue in the late afternoon. The sun wouldn't go down until after 9:00, but it was low in the sky by the time we lined up to be served.

We all had a little, but there had been only enough money to slaughter one cow for the celebration. After the breeding problems, no one was willing to waste anything.

Dancing started about an hour before the sun went down. There wasn't a wooden floor, just ropes and a police railing that closed off part of the smoothest stretch of street pavement in town. "Do you want to dance?" I asked Millie.

"Sure."

We worked our way into the crowd, not to the center, but far enough that you couldn't watch us from the side. When the music changed to a slow song she started to leave before I could even ask if she wanted to dance.

Then Charlie was there again. "Hey, beautiful. Let's dance," he said as he stepped between us. He curved his arm around her shoulder again and guided her back to center floor without giving her a chance to reply. I watched, more taken by surprise than anything else. He embraced her as they danced, and then he winked at me over her shoulder as he squeezed her bottom.

"We're gonna take a five minute break, here," said the band leader as the last note tapered off with a drum flurry and a clang on a symbol. I expected Millie to come back and stand with me, but instead she walked off the other side of the stage with Charlie, toward the shadows behind a tent.

I was determined not to show how much that hurt me, so I turned and walked over to get another Coke.

People milled around in small groups waiting for the band to start again, but I stood by myself. There was no one for me to talk with. Then there was a sudden yell from the shadows where Millie and Charlie had gone. "What the fuck?" It was unmistakably Charlie's voice. "You stupid little bitch." Everyone stared, and Millie walked out of the shadow smoothing her shorts, as though it was the most natural thing, and smiling like she hadn't heard a sound.

The bandleader moved to defuse the tension. "All right everyone," he yelled into his microphone. "Let's have the gals ask the guys this time." Millie took my hand and looked up at me mischievously as she pulled me to the open area where couples were pairing off to dance. There was a fast song, and then the band slowed into a slow song. This time, as the music changed, she held me there. It was her decision more than mine that we kept dancing.

About ten minutes later, I saw Charlie step out of the shadows. I nudged Millie's shoulder and turned so that she could see him. She stared at him, and when she was certain he was looking at her, she grabbed my bottom with both hands and pulled me to her.

If it had been any other girl, in any other situation, I'd have been excited, but I was a tool to send a message. She was telling Charlie, "I decide for myself, when, where, with whom ..." But the message was being sent to me, too.

I kept holding her lightly, as I had been, with no expectations. I didn't understand her game, but this was high stakes. I was in the middle, and I felt I was part of making a statement to him, like Fuck You! I stayed stiff as a board because, if that was what this was all about, it would end as quickly as her lying in bed beside me, and I didn't want to be left rejected again.

We met my parents and went to spend the night in a motel where the four of us shared a room with a double bed and two rollaway twin beds, one for Millie and one for me, all crowded together side by side.

I'd told Ted about the Fourth of July in Valentine, and

invited him to come with us, but he said he had things to do on his place. So a couple days later, I walked over with Millie to introduce him to her. After all, it had been her grandfather's home. I still didn't know who actually owned it or if Ted just rented it.

Ted came out the door to greet us so quickly I thought he had seen us coming before we rounded the last turn. "Hey, Jack," he said, "who's your friend?" I introduced them and explained that Millie was Cy's granddaughter.

"He had a really nice place here," Ted said. "And he kept it in good shape. Pretty much nothing to do when I got here but turn on the electricity."

Millie walked to the front door just like the first time she had brought me here when it was still her grandfather's place. Ted watched. "Do you want to come inside?"

Millie didn't reply. She opened the door, stepped in and looked around. I had only been inside that one time for hot chocolate since Ted moved in. We almost always talked outside or worked in the barn when I came over. And no one would shoot a gun inside a house.

The main room looked very similar to the way it used to look. Ted was a little awkward when Millie started for her room, but then he stepped aside as though he had decided something would be okay.

"Wow," she said when she opened the door. There was electronic equipment all over what had been her desk, and there was a separate new metal table with more stuff.

"I guess Jack didn't tell you I'm a volunteer monitor for the U.S. Geological Survey," Ted explained. "They provide the equipment, and I make sure it runs all the time."

I looked at him quizzically. "I told you," he said sincerely. "I'm sure I did. They have amateurs who run monitors for earthquakes. We're like the volunteers who record what weather actually happens in thousands of locations. It's follow-up for fracking. They know the ground will settle, but they don't know how much or how quickly."

I must have still looked puzzled. "Huh. Maybe I didn't tell you then. I thought I did. But it's pretty simple, I have sensors all over the land." He pulled a chart out of a bin where it folded into a box off a printer. "Take this for example." He pointed to a slight bump in a long line. "That was yesterday afternoon. It was only a 1.5 on the Richter Scale, so you wouldn't even notice it. Might look like you knocked the table and the water shook in the glass—a little ripple—no more."

He looked at the table and then back at us. "This stuff's so sensitive it'd pick up a truck coming down the road, but no one drives big trucks around here except to carry cattle once or twice in the spring and fall."

We went back to the main room. He fed us lunch, and

waved as Millie and I left to walk back. "He's kind of odd, isn't he?" said Millie when we were out of sight.

Cy's ranch became a magnet for Millie. She wanted to walk over there at every opportunity. Sometimes we'd walk only to the creek, and other times we'd go to the top of the first hill where we could see the house and the barn, but not go all the way. Most of the hills had only brown dried grass. There were trees only at the creek bed, and they were pretty sad. We usually walked over late morning and then were back for a late lunch. There wasn't much else to do anyway.

Then there was the day we went right after breakfast and Ted was taking target practice when we got to the top of the hill. "Hey," Millie yelled. "Hey!" until he looked over and saw us. He waved and Millie went on down the hill, slowly, being careful not to fall, and then at a run to keep from falling flat at the bottom. I worked my way down the hill, and she was talking with Ted when I got there.

"He's going to teach me how to shoot," she said as I caught my breath.

"Okay," I said and stood around as Ted showed her how to check that the chamber was empty and how to pull back the top of the pistol to chamber a round. "Keep it pointed away from us," he warned. Millie went through the drill several times. She handed the pistol back to him and he removed the clip and checked the chamber before handing it back to Millie.

"You hold it out with two hands," he instructed. "They say 'pull the trigger' but it's better to squeeze."

Millie watched Ted demonstrate and then he handed her the gun. She held it out, awkwardly at first, but then better after he corrected her grip. "Here. More in front, and not quite so close to your body. You want it way out so your arms catch the recoil and not your face."

Millie practiced putting her hands up and pulling the trigger, "Click." When Ted was satisfied, he asked, "Do you want to try it with ammunition?"

"Sure," she said. Ted set up a bucket about twenty feet away, and handed her a clip. As he had shown her, she carefully put the clip into the pistol and chambered a round. She held the pistol in front of herself, fired, and totally missed the bucket.

"You've got to be careful not to change your aim as you squeeze the trigger," Ted said. "There's a tendency to pull to one side or the other."

Millie fired five more times. Finally, on the sixth shot, she hit the bucket. But I noticed something else. The first five shots all hit the exact same place in the dirt behind the bucket. "I got one!" she exclaimed, but a little too quickly to believe she was surprised. "I can see what you mean," she said. "I kept pulling to the left when I pulled the trigger." She checked that the chamber was empty and passed the pistol back to Ted.

I also caught Ted looking at her for just a moment to try to see what he had missed at first.

"That was fun," she said. "Can we do it again some time?"

"Sure," he answered.

It rained heavily at the end of July. I ran to the barn twice a day to check on the cows and to the chicken house to toss out some corn. Dad checked his pirate water system to be certain some water went down the gully and some went into the cistern. Millie stayed inside and read. After awhile, Mom said to Millie, "I'd love to be reading, too, but there are things you can do to help." Millie was a little taken back, but said, "Sure. What can I do?" Mom always had lots of things to do, so she put Millie to work tying bundles of herbs she'd cut and hanging them to dry in one of the upstairs rooms where the sun made it get pretty hot inside. Rain was good for her herbs she said, but when it was that wet she fretted that they were taking too long to dry. "They'll rot if they take too long to dry." And, revealing her real concern, she added that it wasn't fun to run when it rained.

Dad often made some house calls and let Millie and me ride along. Most of the time he let me drive. Usually we took his old pickup truck since it had four-wheel drive in case there was mud, and we all sat on the bench front seat, Millie in the middle.

The day the rain stopped it was beautiful and the sky was the kind of blue when the dirt and dust have been washed out. Millie wanted to go to the creek between our place and Cy's place. "There'll be water in it, I bet." So we went. Some of the path was pretty muddy. We walked on the grass that had sprung up after just a few days of rain.

The pool on the boundary with Cy's place was full and swirling, and like always, it was only knee deep when Millie took of her shoes and waded in. Then she started to unbutton her blouse. "Here," she said. "Let's swim like we used to."

I took off my shoes and followed her in. She turned toward me wearing just her bra on top, and then she lifted one foot and then the other to remove her shorts. Her underwear was wet and didn't leave much to be imagined, but she didn't care.

I couldn't stop myself from reacting. I'd never seen my mom that undressed, and I'd only seen picture of women's breasts in one of Dad's old magazines called National Geographic. That magazine wasn't around any more. Dad had explained how they were run out of business when they tried to get involved in protecting the environment. He had a book they'd published with artists' pictures of naked women in slave markets almost 3,000 years ago.

"Take off your shorts," Millie directed me, so I did. She splashed water on me, and I splashed back. Then she took my hand, just like at on the dance floor in Valentine and led me into the water. I was wet by now, and my underwear clung to me like hers. She pulled my mouth to her, and as she kissed me, she opened her mouth and pushed herself toward me.

She grabbed my bottom with one hand, like she'd done on the dance floor, and put her other hand between my legs. She seemed to know what she was doing, and I imagined she had done this with the football played in Omaha, too. But as soon as she touched me, she froze. I wondered how she could feel my deformity, but after a pause, she touched me again and I forgot my question.

My small curved part reacted to her in a way that I wanted to hide, but could not. I was embarrassed and immediately sat down in the water to cover myself.

Millie could not have failed to feel what happened through her thin wet clothes and mine, but she ignored it. As I sat down, she lost her balance and stumbled backwards so we both were sitting in the water. She looked at me and laughed. I thought at first she was laughing at me. But she kept on laughing, and I knew it was her own joke, not me, that made her laugh.

When she stood up, every part of her that wasn't already uncovered was outlined by wet nylon sticking to her skin. "I'm getting cold," she said, and stepped out of the water, picked up my T-shirt and put it on. It came down almost to her knees. Then she reached under the over-large shirt and removed her bra and slipped off her pants. It looked a lot like what she'd done with her nightgown a couple weeks before as she sat down on the big rock and watched me, careful to hold the bottom of the shirt around her knees.

I was getting cold myself and stood up. All the while Millie stared at my shorts where the outline of my misshapen penis was way too obvious, even in its softer shape.

"You have no idea how different you are, do you?" she mused and then smiled up at me. "No idea at all."

"I'm sorry," was all I could say. Then I sat on the other end of the sunny rock and looked at the stream. We both sat there, looking at the water and thinking our own thoughts in parallel. When our clothes were dry, we walked home. Mom noted that my hair was damp. "We went wading in the creek," I explained.

She looked at my dry shirt as though to be certain that I knew that she knew there was only one way my hair could be wet and my shirt could be dry, but she said nothing.

After everyone was in bed, I crept down the hall to Dad's book room. I knew exactly where to find the drawing by Leonardo Da Vinci. As I stared at the picture of the body of a man going into the body of a woman, I heard someone breathing in the room behind me. I looked around and saw Dad and knew that he'd seen what I was looking at. "What's wrong with me?" I asked him. "My penis."

"You have a small hypospadias," he answered.

"I know. You told me that. But how odd is that? How weird am I?"

"You're not like everyone else at all. In fact, you're so much not like every other boy your age that you're the closest to normal born in this area for twenty years. Since the epidemic started." Then Dad did what he always did. He launched into a medical lecture. "No one has figured it out. Literally every boy is born with a hypospadias much worse than yours. At first the surgeons tried to fix them all, but the reason there're so many ways to do surgery on hypospadias is that none of them works very well. Some experts think it's a virus, like the Zika thing years ago, but no one knows for sure."

I didn't dare tell him why I'd been looking at his books, and I had only the slightest understanding of what he meant when he said I was more normal. All I knew was that I was different enough to be strange.

After breakfast the next day, Millie sat on the porch and

read Anna Karenina. When I asked if she wanted to go for a walk, she said she preferred to read. I wanted to go back to the pool. I knew the water was going down quickly, and the forecast was for dry, hot weather. In my mind, I could almost feel every detail from yesterday afternoon, and I wanted to be as important to her as she was to me. I'd forgotten all my embarrassment, and just wanted to kiss her again.

But Millie kept reading all afternoon. Finally she turned the last page, closed her eyes and folded her hands across the book in her lap. After a long silence, she said, "What a brilliant ending."

I was happy for any conversation. "What happens?" I asked.

"She steps in front of a train."

"Steps in front of a train?" I thought I hadn't heard right.

"Yes. It was so perfect."

"Did that kill her?"

"Of course."

"The book's about her, isn't it?"

"Yes."

"So why is it perfect to kill herself?"

"It solves everything, that's why," Millie said as though my stupid questions were a distraction from her reading pleasure. "Vronsky left her. She was disgraced. That way she got out of her life."

"That's not out of her life. That's ending it."

"You just don't have any empathy, do you?"

She got up and went inside, and I heard her ask my mom, "Anything I can do to help get dinner ready?"

Millie was up early and out the door going to Ted's before I had finished breakfast. I ran to catch up. Ted was taking target practice like he did every morning. He'd gotten a paper target somewhere, and he had pretty much shot the paper out of the middle of the bull's eye. He nodded to us, and we watched.

Millie walked over to him. "Can I get another shooting lesson?"

"Sure."

Ted watched as she checked that his pistol was unloaded, loaded the magazine, put the magazine in the gun, and chambered a round. This time she hit the target the first time. Then she shot and hit the dirt in a perfect circle around where Ted had set the target.

"Maybe you can help me learn to hold it steadier," she said.

Ted waited until she'd reloaded and then stood beside her as she held the gun out with two hands. "Like this," he shifted her fingers on the grip.

"Thanks," she said, as she turned ever so slightly and leaned her shoulder on his chest.

There was a pause, before Ted put his hand on her shoulder to hold her still as he stepped away. "You know. I've got a better idea, Millie. Can you unload the gun?"

Millie removed the clip and ejected the round in the chamber. Ted went into the house and returned carrying two unused paper targets. "Let's see who's the better shot, you or me."

Millie was caught off guard for a moment. "What do you mean?"

Ted didn't bother to explain, "Come on. Let's see who's the better shot."

Ted put the two targets side-by-side on the little mound, paced back twenty-five steps, and scraped a line in the dirt. "I'll go first."

He took the pistol from Millie's hand. She didn't have anything to say as he loaded, fired six shots all in the bull's eye, and handed the gun to Millie.

"I don't want to. I'm not that good," she protested.

"Don't sell yourself short, Millie," he replied. "You've got too much talent for that."

Millie's expression changed to what I can only describe as defiance. "Okay, you're on." She loaded the pistol and fired six shots into the center of the second target so fast I almost thought it was firing automatically.

"That's a good start," Ted said. He paced back five more steps and they repeated the process, followed by five more steps and then five more until Millie missed one.

Ted didn't gloat. "That's really good. Actually, that'd be extremely good even for an adult." He pointed to the last line about forty yards from the targets, "Next time we'll start here. I think the only reason you missed is your arm got tired. I'm impressed."

That night, Millie confused me even more. After I'd turned off my light, she opened the door and said, "Let's go back to your pool tomorrow."

"It'll be dry by now, or almost so," I told her, wishing she'd said that two days ago.

"You don't know for sure. There was still water in the creek when we came back tonight."

"Okay. If you want."

"I want."

There was a little water left, but only just above our ankles when we waded in, and about ten feet wide. She leaned over enough to scoop water to splash me, but it wasn't much and I just laughed. Millie was surprising me by doing new things that were completely different from any way I'd seen her act before.

"My mom's pregnant," she said, talking away from me, sort of like she was talking to Dad's pump under the bush, which we'd shut off the day before as the water went down. But I could hear her every word because the air was still and there was no other sound. "They were doing it all the time, every time my dad went out of town, for a long time, several years. They did it the old way." She wiggled her toes into the last bits of mud, and she kicked the water to rinse her feet.

"I walked in on them one time." She smiled mischievously. "On purpose. I could hear her making her little noises and I wanted to yell, 'Daddy' like he'd come in the house, but I didn't. I couldn't even make them stop when I was in the room. It was like The Jerk wanted me to watch. She mimicked a high-pitched little girl voice. I just said, 'Oh, sorry', like I'd made a mistake and left."

I couldn't think of anything clever to say, or anything to say at all. But I didn't need to. Millie kept talking.

"When they do it the old way, girls have to worry about getting pregnant, but not any more. A guy only gets you pregnant if he wants to. And if you go along." I'd begun to think the old way was like the drawing from Da Vinci.

As abruptly as she'd changed her mind and wanted to come to the pool, she put on her shoes and said it was time to go back.

I felt I should say something, so I tried to show empathy, "I'm sorry about your dad."

"Oh, he figured them out on his own. The only thing

he couldn't figure out was how to take me with him. He wanted to, and he said he will eventually." She didn't speak for awhile and then added, "My dad's the one who taught me to shoot. He said I might need to know how some day. 'You never know,' he'd say every time we practiced."

Farmers everywhere had the same challenge getting cows pregnant that Dad and Doc Porter'd had. The only solution was collecting semen from bulls, and that was complicated and expensive. The result was that beef cost a lot. Chicken, on the other hand, wasn't a problem, so Mom cooked chicken most every night.

Dad said it was interesting that whatever was going on was in the bulls and the bucks but not the chickens. "Must be something specific to mammals," he concluded.

I remembered that humans were mammals, too.

So it was special when Mom had hamburger for dinner that night. "To celebrate Bastille Day," she told us. She'd studied French in college, and she'd been to Paris on the same trip when she'd been to London. She went on to explain that Paris was at about the same altitude above sea level as London, but it was farther from the ocean than London, so their dike had been more successful and Paris hadn't been flooded, at least not yet.

After dinner, Dad suggested we get out my telescope. Mom wasn't interested, so she didn't climb up the hill behind the house with Millie and Dad and me to set it up. It was a steep hike with a lot of switchbacks, but there was a sort of path that Dad said must have dated back to when the Lakota roamed that area. He'd found some primitive pictures painted on the rocks that he said were very old and proved his reasoning.

It was unusually warm, and the sky was clear as glass. Thousands and probably millions of stars could be seen with your eye alone, and the telescope made it possible to see twice that many. Dad explained to Millie earth's insignificant place at the edge of the galaxy the same way he'd explained it to me. I always wondered if I'd ever know as many things as he did.

After awhile, Dad said he was tired and he went back down.

Millie and I sat there. I was thinking of whether I dared to put my arm around her or try to kiss her again when she said, "I ran away."

"What do you mean, 'ran away'?" I asked.

"Ran away. Mom doesn't know where I'm at."

"Wow. Your mom doesn't know you're here?"

"Not a chance."

She smiled in a way that was proud of herself, "I told my mom so many times that I hated this place and I hated all the summers I spent here with Cy. I said it so many times, this is the last place she'll look for me, if they look at all."

"Then why'd your mother ask if you could visit?"

"She asked because I got a friend to show me how to hack her email. She never called. Remember, she just wrote a note and asked if I could stay. It wasn't that hard to fake."

"But Mom got an ePDF from her. How'd that happen?"

"I told you. I hacked her account," Millie said.

"I don't believe you."

"It's true. All I had to do was figure out her password."

"That'd be impossible to guess."

"Not if you know my mom. She told me our family password one time. It's my name spelled backwards. I guessed her own would be something like that, and it is. It's The Jerk's name spelled backwards. Simple."

"But what if she finds out?"

"She won't. She's convinced I hitchhiked to Richmond." I asked why Richmond, the new capital.

"Because its the new center of everything. They run the glass bottom tour boats to look at the rocks left from DC. It's ironic isn't it? The capital of the Confederate States becomes the capital of the whole country after DC and New York are underwater."

"Do you have friends there or something?"

"No, but Mom doesn't know that. She put me on a

plane once to meet my dad there for a vacation, and I've been talking about my best friend there for two years since I came back. She thinks we're really close. I've been planning this."

When we got back, Mom and Dad's door was closed. Millie talking about her mom and The Jerk made me remember the time I'd walked in on my parents before Mom had me use my own bathroom. I realized they were having sex the old way.

Millie called me softly from her room. "Watch this," she said as she showed me a message she'd typed to my mom on my mom's computer pad. The next morning, when I came down to breakfast, Mom said, "I got a message from Millie's mom. She wants to know if Millie can stay another couple of weeks. She's been feeling ill. I'll tell her 'Yes' if it's okay with you."

"Sure. Not a problem."

"I can't believe you pulled that off," I told Millie once we were outside.

"Talent." She smiled. "Natural talent."

After breakfast we walked to the pool. It had dried, leaving only a small damp area. We picked our way along the bushes. I watched her as she walked ahead of me. I still remembered our kiss just a few feet away, but it seemed less urgent, or perhaps a little out of place after what she'd confided about her parents, and her mom, and all the things she worried about. And making plans to run away from home. She was amazing!

"I keep expecting the drone to fly over any time," I said, just to say something.

"A drone? Like we saw that time before?"

So I explained about the Sioux Falls Water Department.

"It's always someone saying they have rights over someone else, isn't it?"

We went to Ted's that afternoon. Millie and Ted started shooting at forty yards, and were pretty evenly matched up to sixty yards, but at that range both of them started missing. Pistols aren't very accurate at that range.

I shot too and felt grossly outdone by both of them, but they humored me. When I hit the target at twenty yards, even way off to the side, they both cheered; but I wondered if there was a little sarcasm in their praise.

"Where'd you learn to shoot?" Ted asked her.

"My dad," she said.

"He must have been pretty good. Where'd he learn?"

"Army I think. He was an MP he told me one time, whatever that stands for."

"Like you were," I said to Ted.

"Military Police," Ted explained MP to Millie. "Is your dad still in law enforcement?"

"Nope. He travels for some business. I don't see him much since he and my mom divorced."

I figured Ted asked if Millie's dad stayed in law enforcement because he was interested in everything.

He also asked if we wanted to have dinner with him. We said yes, and he called my mom and said he'd drive us back later, which he did. On the way back, he asked, "Say, Jack. When's your birthday, again?"

The moon was up and very bright when we went to bed. In the middle of the night, I rolled over and saw a glow from where the moonlight shown in the bathroom window. Millie was standing in the door watching me. When she realized I'd seen her, she closed my door to the bathroom, and I heard her close her door on the other side, too.

The next day, Mom and Dad went down to Lucy's and then were going to visit some friends before dinner. Millie and I walked toward Ted's place but decided to see if any water was left in the pool. As we got to what was left of the pool, I heard a whir and looked up to see the drone. "Fucking spy!" I exclaimed, and I picked up a rock and threw it. But it was too high and then it circled, like it had before, to prove it was immune to us.

"Here," said Millie, "Let's make the operator really jealous." She grabbed my chin and kissed me hard.

The drone circled as she put her hands down the back of my shorts and rubbed my skin. She stepped back from me and looked up at it as she pulled her T-shirt off over her head and stepped out of her shorts one foot at a time. Standing there, mostly naked, she leaned back so the drone operator got a good look and came closer.

As she worked her way to the far side of the creek bed, she taunted the unseen person behind the controls as she took first one and then the other bra strap off her shoulder. Then she turned her back to the drone so it could focus on her unhooking and dropping her bra to the ground. She looked over her shoulder at the drone before she stood on one foot and then the other to remove her pants until she was fully naked with her back to the drone.

She bent over. The operator had forgotten about me, and the drone came closer.

Abruptly Millie spun and threw a handful of marble size rocks at the drone.

The operator was caught off guard. One rotor jammed, another snapped, and the drone fell. Millie ran to it, grabbed it and held her middle finger to the camera eye before she cracked the third propeller with another rock. "Let him explain that to his boss," she said, "Fuck you, Sioux Falls Water Department." And she crushed the drone open with another rock and pulled out the battery.

I was three times mesmerized: by her audacity, by the accuracy of her aim, and by her nakedness. She looked at me and walked across the mud, barefoot, ignoring the pebbles, and kissed me hard. Her kiss was definite, and her choice.

She reached down and touched me. I was excited. Then she undid my waist and slid my shorts down. I took my shorts the rest of the way off, and she laid my shirt across the big rock and lay down.

"Are you sure you want to do this?" I asked.

She nodded. I tried to remember everything I'd overheard from guys at school. Even the nice guys had ideas about how to have sex with a woman. Go slow. Kiss a lot and then touch my way down to her breasts. Kiss her abdomen, and finally touch her vagina. Sex education in school had been all about reproduction and getting sperm out of a guy's testicle. This was different.

She curled her hands behind my head and gasped as she held my head on her stomach with both hands. I wasn't certain whether her sounds were to tell me to stop or to tell me to go on, so I just stroked her stomach until she guided my hand down. She curled her body a little as I touched her hair.

She took her other hand from the top of my head and reached between my legs. I visualized my deformed hypospadias, pulled half erect in its downward curve like a finger pointing toward her feet, and I knew she was appalled. Instead, she held me. I felt myself pulse. There was thick moisture on me and on her hand, and I was mortified.

I was afraid to say anything, but Millie curled up beside me and put her hand on my shoulder. I started to move away, but she pulled me back, and after awhile we fell asleep.

I woke up an hour or so later. Millie was looking at my face, and then at my deformed penis. "I've never seen a guy who looks like you," she said.

Any lingering excitement I might have had vanished. All I could think of was her football player and any other guy she'd been with in Omaha. "I'm sorry," I said. I'd spent years hiding my deformity, and now I'd been exposed as defective and compared to better guys by the one person in the world I'd ever really wanted to like me.

I waited for her to get up and leave, but she didn't. Instead, she kept talking to me, but as though she was explaining something to herself that she had never expected. "You still don't get it, do you? Not one single guy our age is like you. Every other guy is like your dad's bulls that Cy told me about."

I must have looked surprised.

"Don't be so surprised. Cy talked with me about a lot of things. You're longer. And you have a hole at the end, not in the bottom."

I could feel each word, as though her voice had taken

hold of my head and was holding me on her stomach again. Only this time her hand held my face to look at her eyes. "I took care of our neighbor's baby boy, changed his diapers and stuff. One time I saw my dad, and he's all different from the neighbor's boy." She thought for a moment. "You're more like my dad." I didn't reply, but I wondered how The Jerk would fit into the comparison.

Millie didn't wait for me to comment. She kept talking. "When I walked in on my mom and The Jerk, they were doing something different from what they taught us in sex class, or what the girls talk about anyway. It was like they had a secret way."

She was quiet for a long time. I heard the breeze pick up and knew that we had to head back because the sun was going down. But Millie lay back down and pulled me to kiss her. "Whatever happens," she paused, "don't stop kissing me. You need to kiss me." This time she touched my stomach and rubbed her hand below my waist. Abruptly she sat up, pushed me to lie flat.

I had my embarrassing foot-pointed erection again, but I was more relaxed.

She pulled back and repeated, "Just keep kissing me."

Then she moved her legs apart, pulled me on top of her, and guided my hypospadias between her legs. As she did, she wrapped her legs around me and grabbed me with both her arms around my body as much as possible.

We didn't move. We just stayed as close as possible. Like I was part of her.

Finally, my hypospadias jerked again, but this time there was nothing on her skin and I didn't make a mess. I would have been happy there forever. Millie held her breath, until I wondered if she was okay. Then she relaxed and smiled at me. "Can I keep you?" she asked.

The sun was low in the sky when we woke up the second time. We splashed water from the little pool that was left to clean ourselves before we got dressed.

I didn't want the afternoon to end, so I took her hand and led her to sit next to me on the big rock. The sun had gone behind our hill, but there'd be two more hours of late afternoon twilight. And Millie had more to say.

"The Jerk did more than just touch me," she said, not looking me in the eye.

She let that sit between us for several minutes.

"Mom didn't protect me. She knew, but she didn't protect me. I'd thought about running away since he moved in, but that made up my mind. When she didn't stand up for me, I knew I was on my own."

I didn't know whether to put my arm around her, or if that would be the wrong thing to do—like trying to be close when she didn't want anything to do with any male—but she moved my hand around her shoulder, like the first night when she arrived.

"He drank a lot, and he had to use these pills to have sex with Mom. One time, Mom left me alone in the house, or at least I thought I was alone. I was taking a shower and looked around, and he was staring at me with no pants on. He said he needed pills with my mom but he didn't need pills with me. He pulled me down on the bathroom floor." She talked faster like she was trying to run away. "I told Mom he'd been watching me in the shower. I was too ashamed to tell her the rest."

"When she confronted him, he said that same bullshit: He was doing me a favor because I'd never find a real man if I had to chose from boys my age."

"And that's when you ran away?"

"I had to do something, and Mom wasn't going to help me."

At this point, she almost smiled, but it was the same smile as when she'd thrown rocks at the drone.

"Mom left him with me the same day I wrote her letter to your mom about me visiting. He started to put his hands on me, so I grabbed him and made him come with my hand. Then I offered to make him breakfast. The bastard had so much ego he thought I wasn't angry. I made him an omelet, and I mixed in all the rest of his pills for sex."

She did smile now. "He ate the whole thing. Then he started saying he felt bad, and he got real painful in his crotch. I made the mistake of smiling, and he realized I'd done something.

"He grabbed me, but I poked his eye and got free. He thought I was going to run outside and blocked the front door. But I had enough time to get to the closet in my parents' bedroom and lock that door behind me. That's where my dad's pistol was.

"He started kicking at the door, and I fired at him through it. High, to miss him. He swore a lot, but he stopped shouting. A little later I heard an ambulance out front, and I assumed the pain got bad enough that he called 9-1-1."

"And that's when you ran away?" I asked.

"I guess he didn't tell anyone about me shooting through the door, and I still had to wait to hear back from your mom. I hid in a closet at a friend's house. He's the one who showed me how to hack my mom. His parents work, so I could walk around inside during the day. He got me stuff in a drug store so I could change how I look, and as soon as your mom wrote back, I was ready to go. I was going to take the bus, but I figured people might be looking for me there, so I decided to hitchhike. I got him to drive me an hour north to start from."

"But that means you were in hiding for over a week waiting to hear from Mom." I'd been counting days as she told me what'd happened.

"Yeah. Sounds like a spy story or something, doesn't it?"

As far as my parents knew, Millie's mom would pick her up in a couple of days. That was the first challenge, but it was easy. Millie hacked her mom's account again and sent another ePDF asking—no, begging—for Millie to stay a couple more weeks. Didn't I, Jack, have a birthday at the end of August? Could Millie stay until then?

Mom wrote back that it was easy to have Millie visit, and she thought it was good for me to have someone my own age to relate to.

We laughed, and I said to Millie, "I definitely relate to you." I still had no idea what we'd do at the end of August.

Meanwhile, we acted like everything was normal. We hiked to Ted's. Millie got to be as good a shot with his 0.22 as she was with his pistol. In the morning I usually let her sleep in while I did chores, but I saw her watching me from her window one morning, and then I saw her watching me every morning.

Once as we crossed the creek bed, we saw a drone and gave it the finger. The drone went up quickly and flew away. We gave each other a high five. "Taught them a lesson, didn't we?"

The pool dried hard as a brick. We stopped there a lot of days. I put an old horse blanket under a tree across from Dad's water intake. When we felt daring we undressed and made love. That's what Millie taught me to call it.

At night, after everyone was in bed, she'd come into my room and lie by my side. I loved touching every part of her, but we never had sex in the house, and after an hour or so, she always went back to her room.

We were too young to create an adult plan, and we avoided talking about what would happen at the end of the summer. And then it was my birthday.

The weather report predicted thunderstorms, but it was sunny in the morning and only got cloudy mid-afternoon. Dad made a fire in the barbecue and Mom roasted several chickens. Ted came, and some of the guys from school. Ronnie was six months older, so he said with authority, "You'll now be able to get a real driver's license, if you pass the test."

"No problem," I replied, "but the trip to Valentine will be the chokepoint. Need to find the time."

"Like you're so busy and popular," he said. And we high-fived each other.

Ted spent most of his time talking to my parents and Lucy from the store.

Kobb showed up in late afternoon just after the sun settled over the hill. We could hear his motorcycle idle down our dirt road, across the gully, and into the yard. He joined in and put some sausages he'd brought on the grill. It wouldn't be dark for another hour, but we were in the shade and it was getting cool. To stay warm, he and Dad and Millie and I tossed around a Frisbee.

We beckoned Ted to join in, but he just waved and watched the grill. I also noticed that he kept pulling out his cell phone and punching keys. No one's cell phone worked at our place, but he seemed to think his would.

When we were about to eat, I heard a horse whinny, over toward the path to Ted's place.

There weren't any horses around there.

Horses needed too much water.

Granddad missed his turn catching the Frisbee. As the disc passed his hand, he looked at Ted and Ted looked at him.

A voice over where we'd heard the horses called out with a bullhorn, "Perseus Kobb. FBI."

Granddad hesitated, but only for a moment.

In one continuous motion, he jumped on his motorcycle. It caught the first time he jammed his weight on the kick-starter. He gunned over across the gully toward the road, but red lights were flashing from that direction, so he swung back toward us and the path to Ted's place. Three uniformed horsemen rode up the path from Ted's place, lined up, blocking his way.

Ted called out, "Doctor Kobb, there isn't a way out.

Let's make it easy on everyone." He held up a badge for granddad to see.

Kobb, turned slightly, hesitated, and then rode the only way left open for him. Weaving slightly, as though taking an instant to double check his escape route, he rode under a low tree branch and gunned his bike straight at the hill.

Ted dropped to one knee. He didn't need to chamber his first round before he extended his arms to steady his aim. Terrified, I called out, "Ted!" But he didn't hear me, or he ignored me, and in a kind of slow motion, he fired one shot.

The tree branch splintered over my grandfather's head.

Everything took an eternity. And something inside of me became responsible for itself as I ran toward him. I yelled again, "Ted!"

He fired a second time. The limb over Kobb's head splintered again, this time a little closer to the trunk of the tree. Ted fired a third time. The tree limb splintered another foot closer to the trunk. I was closer, but not able to stop him.

After his fourth and a fifth shot, the limb was still dangling from the tree, but only because its leaves were tangled into another branch.

I caught Ted's arm and pushed it down.

He easily stood free of me, but he didn't seem

surprised. He ejected the clip from his pistol, mechanically, looking me in the eye as he let the used clip fall and snapped in a loaded clip from his pocket.

The riders drove their horses to cut off Kobb's escape. But he'd surprised them and was already going uphill on the bike, grabbing the fuel tank and leaning forward to keep from falling over backwards.

The first horse shied at the bottom of the hill. Kobb was faster and widened the gap.

One of the riders pulled a rifle from its saddle case. His horse was excited, so he couldn't get a steady shot, and when he fired rock exploded close to Kobb, but not close enough to harm him.

Kobb started weaving, then swung left and broke for a ledge that was a little below where he had gotten to, and where he'd be out of sight for a moment. The next shot sent up a puff of dirt beside the ledge, and a moment later Kobb sped back to where he'd been and over the top of the hill followed by shots from all three riders.

Ted yelled at the lead rider, "Go back where you crossed the creek bed. Just over there's a path to the left. Cut him off." He was yelling into his cell phone, too. "Target escaped. Heading north. Request backup and search capability ... over ... got it." He got into his truck and sped up our driveway. Now I understood why he always parked headed out.

As dust billowed behind him, I picked up the clip Ted had dropped on the ground. It had one unused cartridge.

The storm burst on us about the time the helicopter arrived. With the lightning and wind, the pilot said it was too dangerous to do an air search, and hail quickly cut visibility to a few yards in the darkness. They launched a drone, but it was blown into the hill in the first few moments.

The two deputies who'd come in the helicopter had dogs, but they lost the scent right away. It wasn't clear if there was no scent because of the rain, or because granddad left less scent from the motorcycle, or a combination.

Everyone who'd come for my party left really quick, and the FBI people didn't seem to care about them. Mom carried dishes inside. Millie helped her. None of us spoke. When more men showed up in the yard Mom locked the door and turned on Dad. "What the fuck is this all about?" I was startled that she knew the words. Dad was still shocked. "I don't know."

"Well he's your dad," Mom said. "He's been coming in all times of the day and night for years."

"I know," said Dad. "I thought it was some kind of thing getting over Mom. He just walked out of his practice and disappeared. Mom was who he lived for.

She was the only one who ever could calm him down."

"Well, she didn't calm him down this time!"

Dad didn't answer—I don't think he had any idea what to say. Mom started washing dishes, but she was slamming each one down on the counter as she finished rinsing it. It was amazing that none of them broke. "You and your damned peaceful place in the country," she said to Dad after awhile.

"I'm sorry," he said.

"Hell of a lot of good that does," she said back, not yelling, but really definite. "No New York ... No Paris ... Not even Omaha ... Just these fucking weeds." I felt horrible because I'd always felt they lived there to hide me.

Ted came back. The door was still locked, and he knocked. "Sally, Mrs. Kobb, it'll be easier if I don't need to get a search warrant and knock some doors down."

Mom unlocked the door, and Ted came in and questioned Dad. "Why'd you shelter a known fugitive?"

"Fugitive from what?"

"Your dad's a terrorist. Killed a highway patrolman forty years ago."

"Forty years ago? You're wasting time on an old man?"

"There's no statute of limitations on terrorism, especially if it involves murder of an officer."

"My dad's not a killer."

"He blew up a bridge. Did he ever tell you about that?"

"Some guy blowing up a bridge, yes." I'd never seen Dad so uncertain of what he was saying. "But not that it was him. Besides," he tried to speak more definitely, "it ended the drought for six months until they put in a new pipe or something, at least that's what he told me."

Ted ignored the logic of Dad's statement.

"Innocent people don't hide out for decades. They don't take suicidal runs at a hill like that to escape." Ted put his coat on, getting ready to go back out with the searchers. "If you hear from him, let us know. You'll be an accessory if you don't, and there'll be no place to hide for you, either. You've been hiding him. That makes you an accomplice already if I decide to charge you."

"Right," Dad argued back. "An old man shows up here five times in ten years. Stays a day or so. Doesn't tell me anything about where he lives all the rest of the time. I wasn't part of whatever happened. I don't even know what happened besides what you just told me."

The Northern Nebraska Emergency phone rang. Ted told Dad to ignore it. Dad said it only rang for emergencies and answered anyway. "I have to make a house call," he said when he'd hung up.

"You can't leave," ordered Ted.

"Why not? Are you arresting me?"

"If I need to."

"On what charge?"

"Accessory to terrorism."

Dad laughed. "I wasn't born forty years ago. How you going to make that stick?" He grabbed his obstetric bag and headed toward the door. But when he got to it, a new person grabbed the bag.

"Who the hell are you?" Dad asked.

"Galloway. Homeland Security," the man said rudely. "You the guy who's been hiding the terrorist?"

"You guys are a broken record," Dad said. "Now, I've got an emergency to help with."

"You're not going anywhere."

"You going to be responsible for killing my patient?"

"Call someone else."

"No one else will get here. Your pilot already said the storm's too much."

Galloway turned his attention to Ted, "So the FBI muffed it again. Good job!"

Ted held up his middle finger. "We'll catch him."

Dad left while they were arguing.

The rain ended late that night, and Dad returned in the early morning. As the weather cleared we heard, but couldn't see, the helicopter fly its search pattern north and west of the hill.

Then all the officers left the hill and moved east and

then south of Ted's place. I was feeding the chickens and overheard one of the officers say as he was leaving, "Edwards has sensors all over the place. When he checked them, he saw that the guy backtracked through Ted's own place and headed southeast."

"Shit, there's no road there," the other officer said.

"There's nothing there. With a 24-hour start, God knows where he's got to now."

Over the next two days, a dozen agents swarmed through the house. They found Dad's book room. Dad stood in the hall as they thumbed through printed books and papers and dumped them in a big pile. All typed and hand-written notes they put in cardboard boxes. "You can't take that," Dad said as they boxed his computer. "It's my patient records."

"Yes, we can," the agent said. "And I bet they're encrypted, aren't they? We'll need to have the password."

"Can't."

"You will."

"If a judge tells me. Not you."

"We can arrange that."

They found Millie's backpack with a loaded pistol inside it. "Hiding a loaded gun?" said one officer carrying it into our kitchen. "That's not so innocent."

"That's my dad's," Millie said. "He asked me to take

care of it when my mom ran him out of the house." The officer checked the serial number, and indeed it was registered to her dad. But he kept the gun.

The next day, they all left. No one told us why, but we saw on the news that they'd found Kobb's motorcycle hidden at an old shack about forty miles east. "In the continuation of the largest man hunt in Nebraska history," the TV reporter said, standing in front of a well-weathered log cabin closely surrounded by trees, "authorities have found the motorcycle used by the suspected terrorist for his escape."

Kobb's motorcycle filled the screen. The reporter began walking around strips of yellow crime-scene tape. "The bike has been cleaned, stripped of any fingerprints." He pointed to a large, empty space under a lean-to at the side of the cabin. "Officials think he had a car here that he used when he abandoned his motorcycle. There is no official word yet, but unofficially, from the trash and other evidence, he lived here for about a year."

We had a poor signal and could not hear the studio side of the story, but the reporter replied to a question. "Yes, the place is ideally hidden. It's surrounded on three and almost four sides by the river on the boundary of the reservation. In fact, the only thing you can see from here is the road we came in on, the trees, and tribal land across the hairpin in the river. This is a very secluded spot.

"There's evidence that the alleged terrorist cut his hair and may also have dyed it before he left. There are no pictures of him in the last several decades, even on his family's computers and phones."

The loneliness of north central Nebraska descended on me as cold as the cloudburst when Kobb disappeared. I was just getting to know my grandfather, and now he was gone and I'd likely never see him again. I hated Ted for using my birthday to catch Kobb, but I was confused because I was sad that I'd probably never see him again, either. And as much as Millie wanted to hide with us, Mom and Dad, especially my law-abiding Mom, would probably send her back to her mother. My senior year of high school loomed as a series of long weekends without friends.

The day after the police and FBI left, Millie wanted to go over to Ted's place. "It's my ranch," she announced. "At least in five years. Cy left it to me, and me alone."

We took my dad's binoculars and walked to the top of the hill that overlooked the house. There was no activity, and finally we walked down. Little lines in the dirt crossed the yard like someone had pulled up a rope or a wire that had been buried only a few inches deep. They ran in all directions toward our place, but only two went the other way, east from the house. Those must've been where wires had gone to the sensors the agents had talked about.

We peeked in windows. The doors inside were open between rooms and everything was gone, all the electronic equipment, all Ted's stuff, everything. Except there was a paper bag on the kitchen table.

Millie tried to open the front door. "Do you think we should?" I asked.

"It's my place," she asserted again, "and besides, looks like everyone left and took everything."

I picked up a rock. With everything that had changed so fast, I was feeling very brave. "We can unlock it." I smiled, and with that I broke the window, and Millie reached in to open the door. The bag had a note pinned on it addressed to both of us.

Jack and Millie,

I'm sorry it ended this way, but it's the way it began, and I can't change that.

Jack, my two calves need water if they haven't died in the heat. I give them to you.

Millie, rule number one, always assume a gun is loaded, especially if you load it yourself.

Rule number two, never load a gun unless you are planning to shoot it.

The Remington in the closet is for you.

You are both great kids.

Good luck,

Ted

PS. Millie, I know you're a missing person. I have to file my After Action Report this afternoon about the gunshots, but I don't need to mention I saw you until my formal report in 30 days.

The sack contained Millie's dad's pistol, but all the bullets had been removed and rolled around loose at the bottom. Ted's 0.22 rifle was in the closet.

I wanted to leave the calves to die, to get rid of all trace of him, but I knew they didn't cause any of this, either then or forty years before.

I also knew that Ted had chosen not to fire his last shot.

As interest in the news story faded, Mom worried she hadn't heard anything from Millie's mom about picking her up. School was about to begin and life had to get settled. And she was surprised that Millie's mom hadn't called after all the news stories that mentioned us and Ted living on Cy's farm.

That night, Millie logged on and sent a message from her mom's computer that she was sorry to be so late. She'd seen the news stories, but she'd been preoccupied because Millie's stepdad had been ill. She assumed we'd have called if there was any danger, and she promised to arrange a time to pick Millie up next week.

Mom got the ePDF the next morning, but after thinking about it all day, she announced at dinner, "Millie, I'm going to have to call your mom in the morning. She's been sending e-messages, but as much as I like having you here, I don't think she can have you stay here when school starts. You have your own classes."

Millie and I didn't have an opportunity to talk before everyone went to bed. After I was certain Mom and Dad were asleep, I went through the bathroom to her door and opened it slightly. "You awake?" I whispered.

"Yeah." She was crying. "It's just so fucked up. I get away, and then I have to go back."

"I think we need to tell Mom and Dad. Tell them everything."

"No. I'd be too embarrassed. How'd they look at me? I wish I had my gun, or there was a train track around here."

The ghost of Anna Karenina crept into the room. "Look," I said and touched her hand, "we don't know what my parents will do. It can't be worse than going back. We should at least ask them."

"They're your parents. Do you honestly believe that?"

"Yeah, but we've got to get them to understand all of it. Trust me, they'll be on your side."

We walked down the hall and knocked on my parents' door. I opened it slightly, "Dad? Mom?"

Mom heard us first, "Uh? Is that you Jack? What's wrong?"

"I need to talk to you. We need to talk to you."

"What time is it? Can't it wait 'til morning?"

"It's kind of important."

"Okay," she said and nudged my dad, "Percy, wake up. Jack has to talk." Millie followed me in. "And Millie, too, I guess."

So we talked for about an hour. Millie talked about The Jerk, and with coaxing and me holding her hand, she told them about the rape. "Oh, God," Dad said. "Whew. I need to think about how to handle that. Your mom didn't back you up, you say?" Then, as he started to think through the options, "Millie, do you know how to reach your dad?"

Mom seemed to understand how difficult this was for Millie to talk about. "We can stall for a couple of days, can't we Percy?" she asked.

"Yeah. After a whole summer, there isn't that much hurry." But Dad was putting on his doctor hat now. "I need to report this. We can't just be silent. No way this isn't abuse."

Millie gasped. "It'll be all right," Dad reassured her. "I just need to find a way through this. Your mom really didn't back you up?"

Mom stood up and hugged Millie and then hugged both of us. Dad joined us and put his arms around the three of us. "I'm glad you trusted us with this, Millie," he said. "We'll work this out."

Millie and I went back to her room. We didn't try to hide anything. I lay beside her and held her as she sobbed herself to sleep.

Millie got so anxious she couldn't eat. She vomited when she tried to take anything except some weak tea with sugar. Mom coaxed her to try bland stuff, but she was too tied in a knot. Dad called Child Protective Services. I heard his side of the conversation and was glad that Millie was in the kitchen with my mom.

He introduced himself. "Yes, that was around here, but the excitement has sort of died down. " Then he told them Millie's name. "I know she is, that's why I'm calling ... I don't think I can do that. There's a question of sexual abuse ... The stepfather, the mom's new husband ... Yes, a divorce situation ... Yes, the mom knows, but she didn't help her ... I haven't ... She's at our house right now...."

Dad stopped talking for a long time and just nodded his head. Then he asked, "A horse? Is it bad?" I wondered what a horse had to do with anything, and there was another long pause on our end. "Okay, we can do that ... How long? ... What about her dad? ... I'll ask if she has a number or a cell ... Yes, I'll call if I hear anything,.."

When he got off the phone he explained, "They only have one case worker assigned to our area. She fell from a horse and broke her leg about a week ago. They asked if I thought Millie would be safe here for a couple of weeks. I said she could stay with us for awhile."

Dad explained his conversation to Millie, but she was still tied in a knot. She only kept down tea for the next few mornings, but she finally was able to eat some light food in the evening. Mom was really good to her, but I also saw her watching Millie really carefully. I worried that somehow she could see something that would make everything worse. Then for no reason I could figure, Mom asked her, "Millie, have you missed your period?"

"It's late, but it's always odd. Mom says it has a mind of its own."

"How late?"

"Forty days. It's never been that long before."

Millie wretched.

Dad finished a sentence on his laptop before he looked up. "What?"

Dad had Millie pee on the swab of a pregnancy test. The result was positive. "That makes it complicated," he said. "He takes advantage of you, and then you're the one who's hurt. But that also means there's a clock ticking to decide what to do next. I need some expert help."

The closest trained gynecologist was in Valentine, so the next day after chores we drove there in the late morning. Dad had met Dr. Furnough a few times before. Like Dad, he was subsidized to provide basic services in an area with a dwindled population. And like Dad, he saw only a few really complicated cases. Not that anything was complicated about Millie's health, but how she got pregnant was really complicated.

Mom went into the room with Millie when Dr. Furnough took her history. Then she came out and said, "He's going to do an ultrasound to see what the fetus looks like. His nurse is free now, and she'll help him." So the three of us waited. I worried about what would happen to Millie. Dad said he'd have to call Child Protective Services as soon as we got back to update them.

Then Dr. Furnough came out to talk to us. "Millie'll be out in a minute. She's getting dressed. She's a great girl, especially after what she's been through." He paused like he was planning what to say next. "So, Sally, when did you say Millie came to stay with you?"

"In late June." Mom casually moved her fingers like she was counting. "About three months ago."

"And the issue with her stepdad was before she came out here? Is that right?"

"Yes," Dad answered. "Why do you ask?"

"Well, she's pregnant all right." He looked over his shoulder at Millie who had just come back into the room. "Everything looks all normal ... but it's about a six-week pregnancy ... not twelve weeks."

Dad look puzzled. Mom thought a second and then said, "But that's after she got here. Since she's been staying with us ..." Then she turned and looked at me with a sudden understanding. "Oh, my little boy ..."

I didn't get what Mom meant at first. I'd barely gotten my mind around the idea that Millie'd gotten pregnant when Dirk raped her. My understanding wasn't helped by our sex education, such as it was, because there wasn't any discussion of how a penis worked to make a girl pregnant. That wasn't relevant to any of the guys I went to school with. This was a big twist in the story because there wasn't anyone around except me, and I had less than zero confidence, or even the idea, that I could make anyone pregnant.

All this seems laughable a few months later, but at the time the idea that I might be a father was almost incomprehensible.

But Dad caught on almost as soon as Mom. "Oh, my gosh," he mumbled as his fingers, too, involuntarily moved to count the weeks. "What the ...? You're right." He looked my way, but he didn't seem to know where to look. Then he involuntarily glanced below my waist before he intentionally looked me in the eye.

"I am surprised ..." he added. But I didn't detect anger, only, as he'd said, surprise. And perhaps there was a hint of relief that the years of worry about my hypospadias had been unnecessary.

Mom tried to make light of it. "Well that answers the question of what's possible despite the epidemic."

Dad thanked Dr. Furnough. Dr. Furnough's expression indicated he wasn't certain that he understood everything, but Dad assured him that he'd cover all the bases. And no, Millie wasn't at any further risk right now.

The ride home seemed to last a lot longer than three hours. Neither Mom nor Dad had any idea of what else to say, so they talked about anything but Millie's pregnancy. As soon as we walked into the house, Mom said, "This is too much to think about any more right now. Percy, wasn't there a news program you wanted to watch tonight? I'll get dinner on. What do you think?" She turned to Millie like she was taking over because someone had to be in charge. "You can help me."

"Sure," Dad said, partly to Mom, but more to himself. Otherwise he avoided the subject like Mom did.

Once the table was set and dinner was in the oven, Millie and I started to go outside, but Mom said, "Let's have you two stay here for right now. I want to know what's going on in my own house."

"We've never done anything to disrespect your home, Mom. Never."

"Is that supposed to make me feel better?"

My feelings were all over the place, but I couldn't just sit in the kitchen. "Can we sit on the porch?"

"The porch? Yes. But stay where I can see you."

So Millie and I sat on the step to the yard. I was as confused as when she'd told me that The Jerk had raped her. Was I supposed to touch her and hug her? Or would my touch make her feel worse because of what had happened when I was close to her before? But Millie looked at it differently. "What's the matter? You afraid you'll catch something from me? Last time I heard guys don't get pregnant."

"I don't know what to say, Millie. You're so special and well, I ..." I had no idea where that thought would lead. Then I surprised myself. "I love you, and I don't want to do the wrong thing. I got you into this mess, and I don't know what to do."

"You got me into this?" she challenged me. "Seems that I was the one who got me into this. You just happened to be there." Then she added, with her typical mischievous smile and a glance below my waist, "And what a wonderful thing to happen to be there."

That ended any uncertain feelings between us. I put my arm around Millie and kissed her hair. I looked back and saw that Mom was watching us, but she wasn't angry. Mom was staring as though she was remembering something. She knew getting through a pregnancy would demand more skills than two kids holding hands on a porch in the early fall would have on their own.

I got a romanticized idea of Millie and I as two young persons living off the land, but of course that was impractical, or more accurately, impossible to do without help, a lot of help. I knew something about the animals and how to drive a car, but I didn't have skills to earn a living.

Mom and Dad didn't come out directly and say it, but they dropped a lot of hints that being a parent now would end my hopes of going to college. I'd done well on my college exams, but that wouldn't mean anything if I was a new dad.

I knew about abortions, and I'd been thinking about that from the moment the test was positive. I knew that would end the problem, but it would probably end my friendship with Millie, too. So the choices were we'd either end up as a couple of teenage high school dropouts trying to start life raising a kid. Or we'd end up as two separate people who had given up what I think we both felt was a good thing. Neither option was good. The baby was because we'd become so close, and if we ended the pregnancy, we'd end our closeness along with it. "It's up to Millie," I said when the topic came up. "She can keep it if she wants, or we can go to Sioux Falls ..."

"… where nothing is available any more," Dad interrupted. "We'd have to go to Minnesota. That would be a big deal, and we'd still need her parents to agree to that."

"Mom's crazy religious," said Millie. "She'd never agree. She'd say it was God's plan …"

Millie's protest hung in the room, and none of us had an idea.

Except maybe there was a God, and He had a plan.

No one living around us knew it was me, but the news carried the story of a boy born in Nebraska who had nearly normal genitalia. Dad had been tipped that the story was coming, so we all sat around and watched. The studio announcer—the same one who'd talked about chasing Kobb—led off, "Tonight's lead story is about science." He looked at the camera with the most trustworthy expression possible.

"For nearly twenty years, doctors and scientists have been baffled, indeed stumped, by an epidemic of Male Genital Dysgenesis Syndrome or MGDS. Virtually every infant boy in the United States has been born with severe male abnormalities." Across the bottom of the screen the ticker read, "For a detailed description of MGDS Visit—and it listed the station's website."

The reporter continued, "In a breakthrough,

researchers at the University of Nebraska in Omaha have studied the DNA of a boy born several years into the epidemic who has only a very minor form of MGDS. The results provide hope for a cure. For the story we go to the University Medical Center in Omaha."

The screen shifted and another reporter stood beside a woman in a white coat. "Can you tell us in lay terms what you've found?"

"We've long assumed this was a genetic problem," she explained, "but we've not been able to find any mutation, any change in a gene or the DNA." The screen showed test-tubes and hands working, "What's new this time is that we were able to study DNA from an infant born after the epidemic began. We learned there isn't a change in the DNA; there isn't a mutation like we thought."

"So what is it?" the reporter asked.

"It's a change in what we call methylation. There are little groups of atoms called methyl groups. Actually, they're almost exactly the same as molecules of natural gas. Normally the body attaches methyl groups to DNA to change how the DNA behaves. If the methylation is off, the genes don't behave normally, even if the genes themselves are okay."

"How does this relate to the infant in your study?"

"We found that every boy born with MGDS had methylation of a gene we didn't think had any function at all. But the boy with only a very minor form of MGDS didn't have any methylation there. So we found a whole new gene, and a surprising way it could go bad."

"And does this get us any closer to a cure?"

"That's not possible to say yet, but it's definitely a step in the right direction."

The doctors' research on my hypospadias was also what helped Homeland Security find Kobb.

I was so different when I was born that the obstetrician asked my parents' permission to keep the placenta to study why I was so lucky. Years later a research group sequenced the DNA from my placenta and identified two genes that worked differently in me and in the boys who were worse off.

When the researchers were done, the sequence of my DNA was put into a national repository, and there it sat until Homeland Security started random screening of DNA databases. Lights went off on my DNA, but I was obviously way too young to have been responsible for what the other Jack did. The same for dad. He was too young.

But this was too big of a cold case, and Homeland Security wasn't going to give up easily. They found an FBI agent who'd grown up on a farm and set him up with a couple of cows on a small ranch near Dad. That was Ted. Ted worked his way into the community, and eventually one of the neighbors mentioned that my grandfather used to show up unexpectedly riding an old motorcycle that he worked on incessantly.

Kobb was the right age.

People will argue and make accusations for a long time about what caused the epidemic of male genital deformities, but some facts were obvious right away.

Hypospadias is a reminder that for the first few weeks of pregnancy, boys, like girls, are open down below. Every fetus has a little bump of tissue at the front end that can fill with blood and get hard, like an erection. When the opening at the bottom closes off, it makes a tube going toward the bump that becomes a penis. In girls, the bottom stays open, and the bump becomes the clitoris.

Unfortunately, when guys a little older than me started having kids, the gene change—the methylation that caused hypospadias—had become a permanent part of the male chromosome. It was inherited by every boy whose father had that gene change.

In the debate about what caused the methylation, some claimed that the scientists had misled the public and it wasn't the methylation. They insisted it was a virus, like the Zika virus that had caused deformities in the brain. The strongest argument, however, implicated chemicals around us every day.

Executives immediately argued they'd tested every chemical in products they made, but they'd tested them one at a time, and it didn't seem to be one chemical that did it. The most accepted explanation was that hypospadias happened when a pregnant woman was exposed to a mixture of several chemicals at the same time. One of the main chemicals was everywhere in ground water because it'd been used for fracking. The other chemical was one of the fifth-generation herbicide/insecticide combinations that plants have been genetically modified to tolerate. Plants do okay with it. People don't.

Businesses reacted, spending millions to discredit the science by casting doubt, a ploy perfected in the last century when companies argued that science couldn't absolutely prove that tobacco causes cancer. So, if it's only a guess, why deprive business of opportunity to earn money?

Several Midwestern chemical companies attacked the science in court. They supported a lot of politicians, and in return the politicians started using the term "print terrorists" claiming that people who write that chemicals cause human disease undermine American business. When the companies weren't denying that there was a problem, they fought each other over who was more to blame.

No one found a reliable way to undo the damage in an individual. One company advertised that it could demethylate the gene in an *in vitro* embryo, for $500,000 per embryo, but made no guarantees that the rest of the fetus would grow okay.

An investigative reporter discovered that, despite the denials, the CEO of one chemical company had funneled millions of dollars into research on how to make any boy's DNA demethylated, so his sons could be like me.

Dad didn't wait to see if anyone could prove the chemical theory. He had a plan of his own. And his plan was relevant if Millie was going to have a baby.

When Mom was pregnant with me, she had a light period even after I was conceived, so they didn't know she was pregnant until she was in her second month. "But all that time we didn't have a well, and we didn't use water from the creek. We drank rainwater that I caught in a barrel and filtered. No chemicals in that at all," Dad explained to Mom, Millie, and me.

"Whatever it is, it's plain and simple," he said. "Hypospadias either happens or doesn't happen in the first twelve weeks of gestation. It has to be the water."

Meanwhile, the one-month grace period Ted had given us before he'd file his report was flying by. That's when Millie announced her decision.

"I'm going to keep this baby," she said at dinner.

"You don't have to. You're awfully young," Mom said.

"I'll support whatever decision you make," I said. Dad gave me a disapproving glance. "And what about college?" he asked. "A baby will take over your life for a long time."

"You were a resident when I was a baby, Dad. That's a lot like school. A lot of things are possible."

"Possible? Yes. But unnecessarily difficult? Also yes."

Millie stood her ground. "I know what's going on with boys my age. That makes this baby kind of its own miracle. I won't go back to live with Mom. I'd be watching out for The Jerk all the time. But if I have the baby, my biggest fear is Mom would find some way to take over the baby and ruin its life, too."

"The only way you can be free of your mom," Mom said as she thought out loud, "is to be emancipated, like a slave is freed."

"What's that mean?" Millie asked.

"If you're an emancipated woman, then you're your own parent as the law sees it."

"How do I get emancipated?"

"Well, one way is to get married." Then Mom realized what she'd said and started talking about other ways to become emancipated. But I'd heard her.

After the dishes were put away, I searched for

emancipation on the Internet, but it wasn't all that simple. I was sixteen, and I'd need a parent's permission to become an emancipated minor under the law. Millie would need a parent's permission, too,

Her dad was her only hope, and we'd have to go to South Dakota. A sixteen-year-old couldn't get married in Nebraska for any reason.

A couple of days later, Millie took a deep breath as she lifted the satellite phone and dialed her dad's cell number. I stood beside her so I could listen to what he said, too. It rang seven times. She was about to give up, when he answered a little out of breath, like he'd run to answer it. "Hello."

"Dad, it's me."

A long pause. "Good god, are you okay? Mom's been worried sick. I've been worried sick."

"Yeah, I'm fine."

"Where are you?"

My dad had warned Millie this would likely be his first question, so she was prepared. "Dad, Mom still has official custody of me. Is that right? So you'd need to tell her if you knew where I was. Right?"

"Okay," her father said. "I won't ask where you are. Can't tell her what I don't know."

"And there's no obligation to tell her you heard from me, only if you know where I am. Right?"

"I guess so." He was getting cautious. "Are you in some kind of trouble? I'll help you out, you know?"

"I'm not in trouble, but did Mom tell you I ran away?"

"She didn't say that in so many words, but everything she did say was so odd, I wondered...why?"

"Then she didn't tell you I shot your gun through a door, did she?"

"No. She didn't! You shot my gun through a door? What door?"

"The bedroom closet."

"What was that all about?"

She used her stepfather's real name. "I shot at Dirk."

"At Dirk?"

"Not at him directly, but to scare him." Millie glanced at me for support and changed the subject. "Dad, can I ask a big favor?"

"You know I want the best for you, but shooting at Dirk and all. I'll have to know the favor first."

Dad had helped us think up the next. "You remember Dr. Kobb who lived next to Cy and Martha."

"Yes." He still sounded cautious.

Millie continued and got her dad to agree to meet Dad in Sioux Falls, and he'd explain everything.

Since Millie's dad had no love for her mom, he agreed he could at least meet and talk, as long as he wouldn't be obligated to tell her mom where she was. That was his one condition. He said he could come in two weeks, but Millie begged until he agreed to be there Tuesday morning. That was still before Ted would file his final report.

Monday night the four of us, Millie, Mom, Dad and I, stayed in a motel about ten miles out of Sioux Falls. We'd definitely seen too many police movies, because we plotted out the next morning like a bunch of amateur spies.

Dad charged the Tesla, so he could drive it to where he'd arranged to meet Millie's dad at a hotel in the center of town. I had the Toyota. After Dad arrived, my job was to be a quick pickup if there were any problems. But there weren't.

Millie's dad met my dad in the hotel lobby. They talked a few minutes, and then, as they started out the front door, Dad said he'd changed his mind, and they went out the back. They talked in back of the hotel for another ten minutes, then Dad asked Millie's dad to wait while he got the car.

I watched Millie's dad from down the street until Dad drove around the corner and picked him up, and then I followed them as Dad drove in ever expanding loops. I didn't see anyone following them, so I called Dad's cell phone. As planned, he pulled over. I parked behind them, got out of the pickup and gave the keys to Millie's dad.

"Go down that road about three miles," I said, pointing. "There's a park on the right. Park the truck and wait. I'll be along behind you." But I wasn't. I drove the Tesla in the opposite direction toward City Hall. Meanwhile, Dad called a Rideshare to go to the far side of the park.

The plan had been to watch for awhile, to be sure no one was following Millie's dad, before she approached him, but Millie was too excited. As soon as he got out of the pickup, Dad told me later, she ran up and hugged him.

The rest was up to her.

Millie told her dad that she was pregnant and that she'd never go back. "You don't have custody, but you're still my parent. You can give me permission to get married."

"Pregnant? Who's the father?"

"Jack is," said my dad.

"Hey, come on. I wasn't born yesterday. That's not possible."

"Well, yes it is. And that's what happened," I said.

Millie's dad turned to her. "You don't have to get married. You can go back to your mom. I'll try to be around more. You're way too young to be a mom. Way too young." He gestured in a vague way toward her stomach and the baby. "Let me help you take care of this."

"Dad," she asked, "can I get you to promise never to hurt anyone for me?"

"You mean Jack here? Okay, I won't beat the shit out of him for getting you pregnant."

"No, Dad. I mean not hurt anyone because they hurt me."

"What's that supposed to mean?" he asked back.

"Is that a yes or a no? Do you promise me or not?"

"Do I have a choice? Okay. I promise."

After he made her that promise, she told him about the rape. He got furious. "But Dad," she reminded him, "You swore to me you'd never hurt anyone because of me. I don't want to lose you, and I've got a chance to be really happy. You can help me make that come true. That's how we'll win."

Her mischievous side surfaced again, "Besides, once I'm married, I'm not Mom's child. I'll be Jack's wife."

Her father thought for a few minutes before he agreed. We'd asked him to absorb a lot, and decide about a whole lifetime for his daughter, on a September morning that was 38° plus (in the new metric system) at 10:00 a.m.

Mom joined us, and we all went to the Marriage License Bureau. The clerk let Dad sign for me, but she refused to let Millie's dad sign for her until Millie told her she was pregnant. The woman took one look at my birthday on the license application and asked, "Who's the father?"

"I am," I said.

"Not possible," she said. "I know what's going on. Do you think I'm stupid? There's not a boy born in the last twenty years who could get a girl pregnant without help. There are no accidents with someone as young as you." She looked hard at my dad and Millie's dad. "It's one of you, isn't it?"

"No, he's telling the truth," Dad said.

"Well, tell the judge. Let him decide."

The judge was slightly amused at the whole disagreement, but he took one look at me and agreed with the clerk. No guy my age could be a father without a lot of help.

I disagreed.

"Son, you don't convince me," he said. "You'd be a miracle."

"Then it's a miracle," I retorted.

"If that's the case, drop your shorts and prove it to me."

Dad was angry. "Come on. You don't need to do that."

"That's all right, Dad." I reassured my father as I unbuckled my jeans.

The judge's only comment was, "Well, I'll be damned."

As we left the courthouse, Millie's dad called her mom on his cell. "I thought you'd want to know, Millie's in Sioux Falls … No, I don't think she'd like that … No, I don't think her husband would like that … Yes, husband. She's married … you do have custody, but permission to marry doesn't require custody, only an interest in my child's future …"

I could hear yelling from his phone, but I couldn't understand what she was saying. He hung up.

Staying on my parents' place seemed logical. Millie's dad came to the ranch to see it, but he was a city person and didn't stay for long. Besides, he'd already given Millie the best wedding present possible. Dad figured the water in his cistern system was cleaner than most any other water we could get.

Millie and I settled into the two rooms where we'd been on the second floor. We slept in my room and talked about how to make the room where Millie had slept into a nursery. We thought of names, like all expectant parents, and we enrolled Millie so we could start our classes together for our last year of high school via satellite school.

Mom drafted Millie to assist in care of the house. I expected Millie to rebel at what some people call women's work, but I think that was the first time since Martha died that she'd been around a woman, or any family, who wasn't trying to get her out of the way, and I think she liked the homey feeling of it. She was a natural at cooking, which helped. After Dad called cooking one big chemistry experiment, she started changing things in recipes in a way that reminded me of Dad and his efforts to preserve sperm by mixing semen in with eggs.

Dad found a book online on the chemistry of cooking. It outlined experiments with leaving out one ingredient at a time from a recipe or doubling the same ingredient. That led to a lot of really weird cookies and cakes. And that was enough to convince me that the people who wrote cookbooks did know something valuable.

Mom and Dad had said that if I wanted Millie to have a ring, I'd have to earn the money myself. It didn't make much difference when we were watching satellite school on the farm, but when we went to the first class session at the schoolhouse, Charlie made some comments about Millie and patted her bottom. She didn't tell me about that until we were on the way home. I was really angry, but she figured it was his embarrassment after the fair and like her dad and Dirk, she got me to blow it off as long as that was the end of it. It was like getting even with The Jerk, the best way to frustrate him was to do well ourselves. Jealousy is an effective tormenter.

I still wanted Millie to have a ring, to wear it really. Her reaction was that from watching her mom, wearing a ring never changed anything. But I'd looked at Mom's ring for years and felt that was part of a marriage. The way we could get the money was to raise more chickens, enough to sell chickens or eggs. I could drive to deliver them, so Millie and I could have our own small business.

We tried moving over to what would be her farm in a few years, and we spent a lot of time repairing the chicken pens that had fallen apart. But between studying and expecting a baby, that was hard, and after the first frost we brought the chickens back and moved back in with my parents for the time being. There were no other neighbors to call on, and living by ourselves in the winter would be too much for us to manage.

I wondered at times if we'd made a mistake, or more personally, if I'd made a mistake getting married. Certainly there had been the other option not to keep the pregnancy. However, we all were subject to the overwhelming feeling—not just in northern Nebraska but also in Omaha and all over—that everyone was trying to get accustomed to a changed world. It wasn't only the cows and deer that changed. Every part of this new life was different. Millie and I had a stake in what was happening, and even though we were very young, when I considered the alternatives, I thought that the pregnancy we shared wasn't just a pregnancy; it was a promise to all of us that something could get better.

In October, Millie's tummy had grown enough that she couldn't get into her tight jeans. She wore loose blouses, like the baggy sweatshirt she was wearing when I'd met her in Sioux Falls and had thought she was a boy at first glance. We talked about what we would say in a month, or maybe sooner, when we went to the classes every other week and it had become obvious that she was pregnant. The way boys were now, we'd be the only teenage pregnancy anyone had heard of for at least five or ten years.

Dad listened to Millie's growing stomach. He tried to get me to listen, but I couldn't be certain that I heard anything. Dad, though, thought he heard two hearts beating instead of one. We drove to Valentine for Dr. Furnough to do another ultrasound. He was surprised we'd gotten married. I think he thought I was born too recently to be the father the same way as the clerk for our marriage license.

It was twins. One looked like a girl—and we prayed that was the case—the other looked like a boy. We couldn't be certain if he'd be normal, or moderately deformed like me, or badly deformed.

We hugged each other at night, and we were thankful for Dad's clean water system.

And we hoped everything would turn out well.

There's always hope.

Scientific Background for KOBB

It is easy to be distracted by dramatic events such as explosions and to overlook the insidious events that threaten all of us. This is one of the reasons that our generation is rapidly wasting the opportunity to make the world better for our children—or at the least, to keep it safe.

Our air, food and water environment gets more complicated every day. New chemicals are continually introduced, and these introductions—combined with the thousands of untested chemicals already in our environment—mean that we are exposed to unknown mixtures most of the time. We have no reliable way to predict the effects of these mixtures, and what little research has been done is not encouraging.

Male genital malformation (sexual dysgenesis) is relatively uncommon, and there has always been a small number of boys born with hypospadias. However, it is now known that exposure of a mother to manmade chemicals during pregnancy more than doubles the risk that a boy will be born with genital defects; and when hypospadias happens, it creates a lifetime of challenges for affected boys.

Diethylstilbestrol, also known as DES, is the prototype chemical causing hypospadias. After DES was given to many pregnant women in a misguided effort to reduce miscarriages, it was found that boys born from such pregnancies had twice the risk of hypospadias. More recently, researchers have used laboratory research and epidemiology of chemical exposures to link significant increases in hypospadias to maternal exposure to various chemicals, even hair coloring agents.

In laboratory research, chemical mixtures are more dangerous than single chemicals. Mixtures designed to mimic chemicals—as they have actually been measured in human breast tissue—cause breast cancer cells to grow faster. Mixtures of unrelated chemicals have more adverse effects than do the same chemicals, at the same concentrations, individually.

Given the limited availability of informative research, we cannot ignore that chemicals may cause even more injury in the future. The story of Jack Kobb is one possible outcome if contamination gets fully out of control. I sincerely hope this story never comes true.

—William Goodson
San Francisco

With Appreciation

Everything we do is enhanced if we receive help and criticism from others. I wish to thank Cyra McFadden for review and criticism of this manuscript, Laurie King for further criticism and editorial review, Jim Shubin for interior design, Polly Lockman for cover design, Laura Vroman for sharing a genuine photograph of Northern Nebraska, and Steele Douglas for showing my better side in a photograph. I thank my family for their un-questioning support and encouragement. And I praise my professional colleagues who are working tirelessly to learn the ways that environmental chemicals affect our daily health.

The Author

William Goodson is an expert in how environmental chemicals affect human health as well as a physician scientist and expert on the care of breast cancer. A graduate of Harvard Medical School, he has been Professor of Surgery at the University of California in San Francisco, held leadership positions in medical and community organizations, published over 100 scientific papers, and been an invited expert at international meetings in England, Germany, France, Russia, and Japan. In 2008, he received the "Compassionate Caring Award" from the Institute for Health and Healing. He has previously written *It's your body ...ASK*, a patient education book about breast cancer, and *The Blue Eyed Girl*, a novel about the lifelong effects of campus violence against women.